WHAT SONG THE SIRENS SANG

Also by Simon R. Green

The Ishmael Jones mysteries

THE DARK SIDE OF THE ROAD *
DEAD MAN WALKING *
VERY IMPORTANT CORPSES *
DEATH SHALL COME *
INTO THE THINNEST OF AIR *
MURDER IN THE DARK *
TILL SUDDEN DEATH DO US PART *
NIGHT TRAIN TO MURDER *
THE HOUSE ON WIDOWS HILL *
BURIED MEMORIES *

The Gideon Sable series

THE BEST THING YOU CAN STEAL *
A MATTER OF LIFE AND DEATH *

The Secret History series

PROPERTY OF A LADY FAIRE
FROM A DROOD TO A KILL
DR DOA
MOONBREAKER
NIGHT FALL

The Nightside series

JUST ANOTHER JUDGEMENT DAY
THE GOOD, THE BAD, AND THE UNCANNY
A HARD DAY'S KNIGHT
THE BRIDE WORE BLACK LEATHER

* available from Severn House

WHAT SONG
THE SIRENS SANG

Simon R. Green

**SEVERN
HOUSE**

First world edition published in Great Britain and the USA in 2022
by Severn House, an imprint of Canongate Books Ltd,
14 High Street, Edinburgh EH1 1TE.

Trade paperback edition first published in Great Britain and the USA in 2023
by Severn House, an imprint of Canongate Books Ltd.

severnhouse.com

British Library Cataloguing-in-Publication Data
A CIP catalogue record for this title is available from the British Library.

ISBN-13: 978-1-4483-0575-9 (cased)
ISBN-13: 978-1-4483-0576-6 (trade paper)
ISBN-13: 978-1-4483-0577-3 (e-book)

All Severn House titles are printed on acid-free paper.

MIX
Paper from
responsible sources
FSC® C013056
www.fsc.org

Typeset by Palimpsest B
Falkirk, Stirlingshire, S
Printed and bound in Gi
TJ Books, Padstow, Cor

Gideon Sable isn't my name. I stole it. The original Gideon Sable was a legendary master thief, who specialized in stealing the kind of things that others couldn't. Like a ghost's clothes, a photo of the true love you never found and jewels from the crown of the man who would be king. But the original Gideon Sable took on one commission too many and never came back, so I stole his name and identity, and made them my own.

There is a world beneath the world, the underworld of crime. Where all kinds of deals can be made in the shadows, where even the best-guarded treasures can feel just a bit insecure, and everyone has a chance to make their dreams come true. Out on the edges of civilization, the rules run out and everything is up for grabs. There are fortunes to be made, if your nerve holds. And if the monsters don't get you first.

Of course, if you're going to take on the big jobs and the big villains, you're going to need a crew. Special people, with special skills. There's Lex Talon, the Damned, because every crew needs its muscle. He killed two angels, from Above and Below, and made armour out of their halos. During our last heist, to steal the infamous Masque of Ra from a Vegas casino, Lex fell in love with Switch It Sally, who can swap one object for another, from a distance, and never be noticed. They got married in Vegas, because everyone does, and now they're off on their honeymoon. Finally, there's Annie Anybody, the woman who can be anyone at all, and is currently my love and my partner in crime.

Together we can do anything. And we do.

* * *

Every crime has a victim, and someone always gets hurt. So the trick lies in choosing the right crime, to hurt the right kind of people and get some payback for the victims. I steal from the rich and keep it, to teach them a lesson. And to make it clear that no one messes with me and mine.

ONE
Seller Beware

I t was just another hot neon night in old London town as those two well-known faces Mad Mental Mickey and Miss Ophelia Knightly went walking through Soho. Except this was a journey into the world beneath the world, where nothing and no one could be expected to be what they seemed.

On this particular evening, I was the man inside the loud and vulgar display that was Mickey, because there are times when even a legendary master thief wants to be sure his target won't see him coming. The tall blonde vision at my side, bestowing her dazzling smile on anyone who even glanced in her direction, was actually Annie Anybody. We drifted through the over-lit streets like a pair of basking sharks who'd sneaked into shallow waters, hiding our teeth behind a pleasing glamour.

We were on our way to Honest John's Magical Emporium and World of Wonders, and while Gideon Sable and Annie Anybody weren't exactly banned from that infamous establishment, if Honest John's security people did recognize us, the odds were that what was left of our bodies would end up helping to support a flyover. Honest John descended, in every sense of the word, from a long line of career criminals and was something of a traditionalist in such matters.

I'd chosen to be Mad Mental Mickey that evening because he was such a well-known rogue about town, a confirmed dabbler in this and that, and a picker-up of unconsidered trifles when no one was looking. Mickey was the kind of cheerful chancer who could turn up anywhere and nobody would be surprised. He always wore the same Union Jack suit, along with crocodile-skin boots, kid gloves and a gold silk cravat. All of it topped off with a crimson wig and huge star-shaped sunglasses. Mickey had a large and all-enveloping personality, so whoever was being him could be sure people only ever saw the look and the attitude, and not the man inside.

Annie was being Ophelia Knightly because that particular young lady was Honest John's current squeeze. Tall, striking and blonde in every sense of the word, Ophelia was wearing designer black slacks and a white blouse with half the buttons undone, to show off a cleavage that could stun at forty paces. All of it under an ankle-length leopard-skin coat that all but shrieked money. Not to mention stiletto shoes with heels so tall and sharp she could use them to stab someone. Ex-model, ex-actress, ex-pretty much anything that required even a modicum of talent, Ophelia was drop-dead gorgeous and not so much a celebrity as a personality: someone famous because everyone else thought she was famous.

Annie normally preferred to create her other characters out of various aspects of her own personality, using wigs, makeup and her extensive wardrobe. But for this job, I needed her to be an actual person. Fortunately, the real Ophelia was never happy unless her exquisite features were gracing the pages of all the best glossy magazines, so all Annie had to do was duplicate the look. After that, it was all about attitude.

And so we made our way through a series of shadowy side streets that didn't so much have names as reputations, glancing disdainfully at shops that specialized in the kind of goods and services that people aren't supposed to want, but always have and always will. Sin and temptation hove into view on every side, readily available at knock-down prices and only slightly shop-soiled. Candy-coloured neon blazed against the night, hot and inviting as a succubus's smile. Most of the people we passed barely acknowledged us, preoccupied as they were with their own imminent damnation, but Ophelia and I stepped it out as if we owned the whole area and were thinking of renting it out as an abattoir for endangered species. Just for the fun of it. Downmarket gods, slumming it among the mortals.

I had intended to work this job on my own, but Annie returned home unexpectedly early and caught me in mid-transformation to Mad Mental Mickey. One hurried and somewhat embarrassed explanation later, Annie insisted on dealing herself in. And since she had just as much reason to hate Honest John as I did, I didn't have the heart to refuse her.

I'd put off taking my revenge on Honest John for some time because I'd been busy, but just recently Annie and I had taken over what used to be Old Harry's Place. There have always been tales about strange magical shops that aren't always there, selling weird and wondrous items that can't be found anywhere else. Old Harry's Place was a pawn shop that was always there and always open. You could find everything you ever dreamed of in Old Harry's Place, as long as it was clearly understood that obtaining your heart's desire wasn't actually guaranteed to make you happy.

Some said Harry was a demon let out of Hell on day release, to tempt the weak-willed with his marvellous merchandise. Others claimed he was the advance guard of a subtle alien invasion, undermining our economy one bad deal at a time. And some said he was the Spirit of Capitalism personified, gone feral. There were a great many stories about Harry, and most of us thought they probably originated with Harry himself, to distract us from getting at the truth.

Harry had recently retired and returned to wherever it was he came from, after emotionally blackmailing Annie and me into taking over his business. Which might have been a kindly deed on his part – or might not. It was hard to tell about things like that, where Harry was concerned. Our problem was that when he disappeared, he took his stock with him, leaving nothing behind but an empty shop. Annie and I were in urgent need of some seriously impressive wares, if we were to continue the business in the style its reputation demanded.

And the best way to acquire such marvellous merchandise in a hurry was to steal it. The best target had to be a similar magical shop, belonging to someone Annie and I had good reason to loathe. Honest John's Magical Emporium and World of Wonders ticked all the right boxes.

It was the kind of place where the prices were affordable, the goods were dubious, and buyers shouldn't so much beware as take out insurance before they entered his establishment. Honest John dealt in the kind of items where curses came as

standard, and the batteries could always be expected to run
out at the worse possible moment . . . but Annie and I weren't
interested in such bread-and-butter merchandise. We wanted
Honest John's Secret Stash: a private collection of the really
good stuff that he kept locked away in a separate and very
well-guarded location somewhere out the back. And since I
always made it a point to keep up with all the latest gossip
and bestow generous bribes on all the right people, I knew
not only where to look for this particular treasure trove but
how to get past its very dangerous guardians.

Mad Mental Mickey and Ophelia Knightly were on their
way to Honest John's sleazy discount warehouse, to rob him
blind. Because he was a complete and unrepentant scumbag,
who had cheated and ruined a great many people, including
Annie and me. It was finally time to make him pay for his
many sins and make ourselves rich in the process. Which was,
after all, what we did.

Honest John didn't set out to destroy Annie and me, but he
did give both of us a good kicking when we were down and
at our most vulnerable. After we had to go on the run from
Fredric Hammer, the worst man in the world, because a heist
had gone horribly wrong, Honest John sold me a cloak that
was supposed to make me psychically invisible so Hammer's
people couldn't find me, but it turned out to have psychic
holes in it. He also sold Annie a new face to hide behind, but
it fell off after only a week. Left exposed to our enemies, we'd
had no choice but to disappear into very deep holes and pull
them in after us, and it took us a long time to put our lives
back together again.

The location of Honest John's magical shop was always
shifting. Either because he was dodging his creditors or because
he thought it helped enhance his establishment's reputation.
(If it's that hard to find, it must be worth tracking down.) You
could only gain access through a dimensional door, a shortcut
between places that was usually hidden away inside someone
else's shop. Like a cuckoo's egg in another bird's nest, or a
werewolf in sheep's clothing.

I had already stolen this evening's password. Annie asked
me how, and I told her she didn't want to know. She just

nodded. Annie was always ready to take my word in such matters.

'Are you sure the real Ophelia isn't going to suddenly show up and ruin everything?' she said abruptly.

'Not a chance,' I said. 'The real deal is currently swanning around Paris, showing herself off at fashion shows.'

'Then won't people be surprised to see her here?'

'Ophelia is a law unto herself,' I said. 'Just like Mickey.'

Annie nodded slowly. 'I didn't know Mad Mental Mickey was one of your disguises.'

I had to smile. 'He's sort of a house name for supernatural criminal types. A useful false face to show the world when you don't want people to know who's really involved.'

'So Honest John will know you're a front . . .'

'But not whose front. I could be anybody.'

'No,' said Annie. 'That's me.'

I consulted my very special compass, which always points to what I need, and it showed me the way to an unimpressive little storefront whose fly-specked window offered untrackable phones, an interesting collection of professional ID cards and a holistic massage service. All of which might have been perfectly legitimate businesses, but no one would bet on it. Most Soho businesses prefer to hide their true nature behind a misleading face. It makes it easier for them to pack up and move on at a moment's notice.

Annie and I breezed into the somewhat undersized lobby as though we had personal invitations, and I smiled and nodded briskly to the cold-eyed receptionist behind the no-nonsense desk.

'Can I help you?' she asked, in a tone that suggested she seriously doubted it.

'Mad Mental Mickey, big and loud and seriously proud,' I said grandly. 'Here with Miss Ophelia Knightly to take in the marvels and wonders of Honest John's business experience and dispense serious amounts of cash in all directions. Today's password is *Swordfish*!'

The receptionist must have hit a concealed buzzer because two large and muscular gentlemen, in ill-fitting suits that looked embarrassed to be seen in public with their owners, made a sudden appearance through a side door. They could have come straight from central casting or Thugs R Us, ready for trouble and more than happy to start some if there wasn't any. They relaxed a little as they recognized Mickey, because he was a known quantity and something they thought they could handle. But then they took in Annie as Ophelia, and all the confidence went out of them. The larger of the two addressed her uncertainly.

'Miss Ophelia? We were given to understand that you were off gallivanting in foreign parts?'

'I was,' Annie said regally. 'I got bored.'

She hit the security guards with her dazzling smile, and they both nodded quickly. They weren't about to get themselves in trouble by arguing with the boss's girlfriend. But I could see that Mickey's presence still troubled them, given his reputation for being a bit of a bad boy.

'Relax, breathe easy and unclench, my oversized brethren,' I said. 'I am currently bodyguarding Miss Knightly, while she diverts and indulges herself in a little retail therapy. An outing entirely approved by Honest John himself, as I'm sure he'll be only too happy to confirm. If you feel like bothering him.'

The muscle boys still didn't seem too certain, so Annie hit them with the full pout and narrowed eyes.

'Mickey is with me,' she said loudly. 'Now let us in. Or I'll tell my sweetie you were mean to me.'

The guards looked to the receptionist, who inclined her head briefly. They all knew when someone had just slapped down a trump card. The receptionist hit another concealed button, and a dimensional door slipped into existence with professional ease. Tall and upright and perfectly ordinary-looking, it stood alone and unsupported at the back of the lobby. Like an actor who'd just cleared his throat so the audience would look in his direction. Annie and I bore down on it with easy smiles, and the door swung open on its own. We strode through with an air of calm superiority and our noses stuck firmly in the air.

A moment later, we were walking down a long, narrow corridor with grubby stone walls and a worryingly low ceiling. Bare arms protruded from the walls at regular intervals, holding up flaring torches to light our way. It was all very impressive, but I knew for a fact that these particular arms were being provided by out-of-work actors, picking up a little pin money on the side. The corridor finally ended in a closed door, in front of which sat a figure clad all in grey, slumped on a stool. She raised her head slightly as we approached her, and all my back muscles clenched.

Annie leaned in close, so she could murmur in my ear. 'Who or what is that?'

'That is the gorgon Medea,' I said. 'One of Medusa's less celebrated cousins.'

Annie shook her head slowly. 'You didn't say anything about a gorgon.'

'You didn't ask.'

'Shouldn't we have brought a shield, to see her reflection in? And possibly hide behind?'

'I think she's probably caught on to that trick by now.'

'Tell me you've got a plan.'

I showed her my most confident smile. 'I've always got a plan. And this one is crystal clear.'

Medea was short and slight, with a face like a silent movie star, all hollows and shadows. She had a spooky if somewhat faded glamour, and her eyes were hidden behind industrial-strength sunglasses. Her long grey robe hung about her in unflattering billows, spotted with recent food stains. A silk scarf covered her hair, bulging out here and there as the snakes stirred restlessly. Medea sat solidly on her seat, as though she had protected her post for ages without complaint and was perfectly happy to sit there for ages more. The gorgon was Honest John's unsleeping watchdog, and no one had got past her in living memory. But then she'd never met Gideon Sable. She leaned forward a little, as though to get a better look at Annie and me, and for all my confidence in my plan, I still had to fight down an urge to take several steps back. I took off my sunglasses and slipped them into my jacket pocket. I didn't want her thinking I was trying to compete.

According to the gossip I'd heard, once Medea had turned unwanted visitors into stone statues, Honest John would then sell them on as lawn ornaments. Unless they happened to be people who had seriously annoyed him, in which case he smashed them into rubble with a sledgehammer. Sometimes he sold tickets.

'Greetings, oh glorious goddess with the wriggling hair,' I said loudly. 'Mad Mental Mickey salutes you, accompanied by the lovely and very well-connected Miss Ophelia Knightly.'

'Knock it off,' said Medea in a low growly voice. 'You're Gideon Sable and Annie Anybody. Did you really think you could con your way past me?'

'Well, that was the plan,' I said. 'How were you able to see through our disguises?'

Medea indulged herself with a brief but disturbingly sinuous shrug. 'I see what is; the better to turn it into something else. I once had a friend who could turn people into pigs, but stone is more permanent. All you need to know is that I can see everything that exists with complete clarity.'

'Good,' I said. 'I was counting on that.'

Before my last heist, the gypsy seer Madam Osiris had presented me with a crystal eyeball, to help me steal the Masque of Ra from a casino in Las Vegas, and I never did get around to giving it back. When I looked through the crystal ball, I could see through all illusions, just like the gorgon. Medea had to make eye contact with me for her transformation spell to work, and as she lifted her hand to her sunglasses, I produced the crystal ball from my jacket pocket. The gorgon removed her shades with a dramatic gesture, revealing eye sockets crammed full of crackling energies. It was like staring at a lightning bolt that was heading straight for you.

I yelled for Annie to close her eyes, squeezed mine shut and thrust the crystal ball at Medea. Her gaze went automatically to the threatening object, and her petrifying glare slammed up against the potent energies locked inside the crystal ball. And for all the power in Medea's terrible gaze, it was an old-time enchantment, while the ball had been recharged only that morning. The gorgon's magic rebounded from the crystal eyeball and turned Medea to stone.

I heard her start to say something she never got to finish, and then it was suddenly very quiet. I opened an eye and took in the squat grey figure sitting on her stool. It looked as if it had been carved out of granite rather than stone, and not one part of it moved. Including the snakes. I let out a breath I hadn't realized I'd been holding, opened both my eyes and assured Annie that she could do the same. She studied the still figure carefully and then nodded briskly.

'Solid work. What are we going to do with her?'

'Nothing,' I said. 'Just leave her where she is. Everyone else will assume she's supposed to look like that, and they'll pass on by. Probably more than a little relieved at not being challenged. By the time someone realizes what's happened to her, you and I will be long gone.'

'If all goes well,' said Annie.

'Trust the plan,' I said.

The crystal eyeball felt uncomfortably warm in my hand. I held it up before me and discovered the entire surface was overlaid with a spider-webbing of fine cracks, from where it had absorbed the impact of the gorgon's gaze. When I tried to look through the ball, it was occupied by a miniature lightning storm. I showed it to Annie, and she shuddered quickly.

'The magic of the gorgon's gaze. How long do you think a crystal that small can contain that much power?'

'Beats the hell out of me,' I said. 'So we'd better get a move on.'

I dropped the eyeball into my pocket, and then we took it in turns to squeeze past the motionless figure on its stool. I tried the door, but it was locked. I pronounced the day's password, but the door ignored me.

'What's wrong?' Annie said sweetly. 'Losing your touch?'

'Medea must have had her own special word, to let the approved customers through,' I said. 'I probably should have asked her what it was before I turned her into a granite promontory.'

'You didn't think this through, did you?' said Annie.

'I was a bit pushed for time,' I said defensively. 'The opportunity to hit Honest John came out of nowhere, and I didn't want to miss it.'

'So what do we do now?' said Annie. 'We can't go on, and we can't go back. We're screwed!'

'Well, to start with,' I said, 'we don't panic.'

'I am not panicking! I am merely expressing a reasonable concern over our chances of seeing tomorrow!'

'Take it easy,' I said. 'There's an obvious way for us to get past the door.'

'Really?' said Annie. 'And what might that be?'

'I think that blonde wig is getting to you,' I said. 'This is a locked door, and a lock is just a mechanism. Use your gift.'

Annie had the grace to look a little abashed. Some time ago, she acquired a gift that made all machines fall in love with her and ready to do anything to please her. Basically, it was a love charm that had gone wrong, but she did get a lot of mileage out of it. She leaned in close for a better look at the lock.

'I don't know, Gideon . . . It's a very simple mechanism.'

'All the easier for you to fool. Don't you want revenge on Honest John, for what he put you through?'

'You know I do,' said Annie. She raised her voice and addressed the lock. 'Open sesame. Please.'

The lock made a loud, satisfied noise as it turned, and the door swung open. Apparently, even a basic lock just lived to make Annie happy, when she turned on the charm. We hurried through the door, and, just like that, we were inside Honest John's Magical Emporium and World of Wonders.

Which was just a big warehouse, packed full of all kinds of goods piled up and laid out in long rows, under unforgivingly fierce fluorescent lights. There was nothing magical about the place; it was really nothing more than a bargain basement catering to the downmarket end of the magic trade. We joined the eager shoppers wandering up and down the narrow passageways separating wooden trestle tables heaped with magical bric-a-brac. I ran my eyes over a few things, just out of professional curiosity, but couldn't see anything worth getting excited over. But then I wasn't the kind of person who would shop in a place like this. Unless I absolutely had to. Which was probably what everyone else was thinking. Most people only go to a place like Honest John's because life hadn't worked out the way they thought it would. Annie and I strolled through the cut-price treasure trove, and no one paid us any attention.

They were all far too busy searching for diamonds in the mountains of tat and trash.

Annie sniffed loudly. 'I'm not seeing anything that could pass for a Secret Stash.'

'Well, the good stuff was hardly going to be left out on open display, was it?' I said. 'Not to worry; I still have my compass.'

'But how are we going to smuggle it all out?' said Annie. 'Hide bits and pieces under our clothes and sneak them past the guards, until we've got enough to fill a moving van or weigh down a fleet of pack mules?'

I smiled patiently, because it was either that or raise my voice, which was never a good idea with Annie.

'How do you think Honest John transported all of this junk into the warehouse? He has his very own personal teleporter: Tommy Two Way. A man who can believe something isn't where it is but is actually somewhere else. Until, suddenly and dramatically, it is. All we have to do is get him on our side, and he can transport the entire Secret Stash directly into our shop.'

'He sounds a bit like Switch It Sally,' said Annie.

'Where do you think she got her talent from?' I said. 'She stole it from Tommy. At least, she likes to think she did. Actually, Tommy let her take a little of his power because he was fond of her. Don't tell Sally; it would only hurt her pride.'

'All right,' said Annie. 'Where is this very talented teleporter? And how are we going to persuade him to turn on Honest John? Tell him, "Sally says hi"?'

'Tommy Two Way isn't exactly a valued employee,' I said. 'John keeps him imprisoned in the same storeroom as the Secret Stash, held in place by a length of enchanted steel chain that anchors Tommy in Space and Time, so he can't teleport himself out.'

'Can we get him out?' said Annie.

'I'm not sure how much power the chain actually has over Tommy,' I said. 'Ever since his wife and children were killed in a car crash last year, I don't think he cares much where he is. But I have good reason to believe that Honest John arranged the crash that killed Tommy's family, just so John could have his very own personal teleporter.'

Annie looked at me sharply. 'Are you sure about this? Because if you tell Tommy that's what happened and you're wrong . . .'

'I am not wrong,' I said. 'Remember Fast Times Larry? He made a dying declaration about his involvement in sabotaging the car, just before the Damned killed him.'

Annie shook her head. 'We're not just here for the Secret Stash, are we? This is about bringing the hammer down on Honest John.'

'Because he deserves it,' I said.

'I'm not arguing,' said Annie. 'All right, what happens after we tell Tommy the truth?'

'I will use the energies in my time pen to short-circuit the chain and break him free.'

'What if the pen can't break the chain?'

'Then I'll just have to improvise.'

'You are very good at that,' said Annie.

We wandered on, looking at this and that, while carefully keeping our opinions to ourselves. Security guards hovered everywhere, guns at the ready, looking as if they were just waiting for an excuse to cut loose and make an example of someone. The crowds of bargain hunters did their best to pretend the guards weren't there, concentrating on searching for pearls among the swine or at least something worth buying.

I wasn't impressed by any of the supernatural flotsam and jetsam set out on display. Wishing rings with barely enough power to nudge the odds in the owner's favour. Invisibility cloaks that looked like quantum moths had been at them. Grimoires with missing pages, objects of power with no instruction manual, and a whole row of unlabelled magic potions. *Try your luck!* the sign said. *Who knows what might happen?* All the usual unnatural bric-a-brac that washed up in the less regarded corners of the hidden world. I didn't know how Honest John could offer any of it for sale with a straight face. Well, actually, I did know; it was because the man had no heart and no conscience. Which made what I had planned for him all the more satisfying.

Huge signs everywhere announced that we were all lucky enough to be present at yet another of Honest John's legendary Grand Sales. *Everything Must Go! Amazing Offers, Astounding Prices!* said even more signs. I'd been careful to time our arrival so that it would coincide with the sale, so I could be sure of a good-sized crowd for Annie and me to take advantage of. Appearing as Mad Mental Mickey and Ophelia Knightly would help keep the flies off, but it wouldn't fool the guards for long. All it would take was one phone call to Paris, and the people in charge of security would know the Ophelia they were looking at was a fake. And then men with really big guns would come plunging through the crowds, to haul Annie and me away for questioning. Somewhere private and discreet, where the crowds wouldn't be able to hear our screams. But I knew from the start that our disguises would only get us so far. I had a plan. In fact, I had several. I kept an eye on the compass concealed in my hand, and the moment the needle finally pointed to the Secret Stash, I stopped dead and raised my voice to address the crowd. Everyone's head came up as Mickey cut through the general babble. Because Mickey is always good for a laugh.

'Greetings and salutations, esteemed ladies and gentlemen and others! Welcome, one and all, to Honest John's Grab Whatever You Can Carry Away Day! Yes, that's right, you lucky people, today is the day all your dreams come true! Just help yourselves to whatever you fancy, and whoever makes it to the exit first wins a fabulous prize! Go for it, my fortunate friends, and grab yourselves a bargain!'

Every single person there believed me. Partly because Mad Mental Mickey can be very persuasive, but mostly because they wanted to. Men and women with happy smiles and fires in their eyes fell on the piled-up merchandise like locusts, filled their arms with as much as they could hold and then charged for the exit. The few guards stupid enough to get in their way were quickly knocked off their feet and trampled underfoot.

And while everyone else was preoccupied with the madness of crowds, Annie and I quietly followed the compass to an unobtrusive side door, currently left unguarded as the security

forces struggled to restore order. It wasn't locked, and I quickly
bustled Annie through and closed the door behind us. The roar
from the over-excited crowd and over-extended guards was
quickly shut off, and it was suddenly very calm and very
peaceful.

Annie and I hurried down another narrow corridor, leading
to another door, although at least this time there was no one
ominous sitting in front of it. I looked quickly around for
surveillance cameras and security alarms, but there didn't seem
to be any. Anywhere else, this would have suggested serious
over-confidence on someone's part, but I knew what was
waiting for us.

'I'm not seeing another monster on guard,' said Annie.

'It's waiting on the other side of that door,' I said.

She looked at me. 'Exactly what kind of magical unpleas-
antness that you haven't told me about are we going to be
facing?'

'Something dangerous enough to make a gorgon wet itself,'
I said.

'Wonderful,' said Annie. 'Tell me you have a plan.'

I smiled. 'I always have a plan.'

The door at the end of the corridor wasn't locked either,
because no one thought it needed to be, and we passed quickly
through and into a room filled from wall to wall and from
floor to ceiling by the single largest turtle I had ever seen. It
loomed over us, a dinosaur among turtles, the top of its shell
scraping against the ceiling. Two huge dark eyes considered
Annie and me thoughtfully.

'That . . . is big,' said Annie. 'Really and quite unsettlingly
big. What do we do now?'

'According to the information I stole along with today's
password, there's another dimensional door on the far side of
the unfeasibly large turtle,' I said. 'Leading directly to the
Secret Stash.'

Annie considered the turtle carefully. 'It shouldn't be too
difficult to get past. I mean, yes, it's big, but what is it going
to do? Lumber forward and sit on us?'

'Unfortunately, this isn't just a giant turtle,' I said.

'If it isn't, it's a really convincing illusion.'

'This is a chronovore,' I said. 'A creature that eats Time. It leeches away all your tomorrows and absorbs them, so it can live for ever. How else do you think it got to be that ancient and that big?'

'OK . . .' said Annie. 'You had better have an astonishingly good plan, Gideon, because I'm too young to die old.'

'Well,' I said. 'I don't know if it's an astonishing plan, but it does have the advantage of being exceedingly sneaky.'

Annie nodded quickly. 'Sneaky is good. I like sneaky. I think we should definitely go with the sneaky, because I really don't like the look that thing is giving us. How the hell does a turtle eat people's lifetimes?'

'All turtles have that ability, to some extent,' I said. 'That's why some of them have been able to live so long – because they're unobtrusively leeching years of life from everything around them.'

'This is not the time for a nature lecture!' Annie said sharply. 'Is that thing already eating our futures? Because I can definitely feel wrinkles coming on.'

'Breathe,' I said kindly. 'Something that size thinks as slowly as it moves. Since we're not trying to attack it, or edge past it, the turtle is probably still trying to decide whether or not we're supposed to be here. So try not to make any threatening movements.'

'I can honestly say the thought had never occurred to me,' said Annie. 'So . . . how are we going to get past this thing without losing all the sand in our hourglasses?'

I grinned and took out my crystal eyeball. 'I've got my eye on him.'

Annie looked at the ball and then at me. 'How is that thing going to help us?'

'It contains the petrifying power of the gorgon's gaze,' I said.

'OK . . .' said Annie. 'That might just work. How are you going to unleash this power?'

'Haven't a clue,' I said. 'This is where the plan collapses and wild improvisation takes over. Along with a certain amount of prayer.'

'Oh God,' said Annie.

'That's it!' I said. 'Now cross your fingers, toes and anything else handy, and hope Somebody Up There has a fondness for big-hearted rogues.'

I took a step forward and thrust the crystal eyeball at the chronovore's face. The turtle saw the sudden movement as a threat and focused its Time-devouring gaze on the eyeball. The finely scarred exterior of the crystal collapsed under the temporal pressure and exploded, releasing all the stored power of the gorgon's gaze. The sizzling energies leaped out to attack what was in front of them, and, just like that, the room was suddenly filled with one very large statue of a turtle.

'Can I open my eyes now?' said Annie.

'If you like,' I said.

Annie took in the giant stone turtle. 'OK . . . very well done, and prizes for original thinking, but don't hurt your arm clapping yourself on the back just yet. The chronovore might not be a threat any more, but how are we supposed to get past it?'

She had a point. We tried edging around the statue, but there wasn't enough room. We tried climbing over the turtle, but its shell brushed against the ceiling, blocking our way, and we were forced to climb back down again. I stood before the turtle's massive stone head and leaned one elbow on it while I had a bit of a think.

'How did Honest John get the turtle in here in the first place?' said Annie.

'Tommy Two Way, of course,' I said. 'Though I'll bet it gave him a hell of a headache afterwards. Well, if we can't go round it or over it, we'll just have to crawl underneath.'

'After you,' said Annie.

The turtle's bow legs allowed us a certain amount of clearance under the belly of the beast. We got down on all fours and crawled across the floor, but soon we were forced to lie down flat and drag ourselves along, with the bulge of the stone belly pressing against our backs. Squeezed and crushed between the floor and the turtle, we scraped along inch by inch. Sometimes our clothes would ruck up and hold us in place, and then all we could do was empty our lungs of air, to give us a little extra clearance so we could try again. Eventually, we emerged from under the turtle's arse, helped each other to our feet, and then took it in turns to give the stone backside a good hard kick, just on principle. This resulted in a certain amount of bad language and some discreet hopping on one foot, before we turned to face the dimensional door that led to Honest John's Secret Stash. The door was, of course, very thoroughly locked, although there wasn't any sign of a keyhole. I tried the password again, but the door didn't want to know.

'Are you sure you've got the right word?' Annie said sweetly. 'Only it doesn't seem to be doing much for us.'

'Of course it's the right word,' I said. 'The receptionist in the lobby accepted it. It just doesn't seem to apply to doors.'

'You had better have another seriously sneaky plan, because I am not crawling all the way back under that damn turtle,' said Annie, very firmly.

'We won't have to,' I said. 'The door must have a hidden lock, and that puts the ball back in your court. Charm the damned thing, and let's see if it will roll over on its back and wave its legs in the air for you.'

Annie unleashed her gift, and the door couldn't unlock itself fast enough. It swung back before us, and we hurried through, accompanied by a low purr of contentment from the door, delighted to have been of service to Annie. There are times when her gift spooks the hell out of me. The door closed itself behind us, and finally we were face to face with Honest John's Secret Stash.

Pile upon pile of the really good stuff, mountains of wonders and marvels, all of it crammed into one really big room. No shelves or display cases, no attempt at categorizing or showing things off to their best advantage; it had all just been dumped wherever there was space, like the contents of an old aunt's attic.

There were no overhead lights; so much of the Secret Stash glowed or glimmered with its own mystical light that the room was illuminated by the hoard's own marvellousness. Annie and I stood and stared for a while, drinking it all in.

'How does Honest John ever find anything when he wants it?' Annie said finally.

I shrugged. 'I don't think he bothers. It's enough that he owns all the pretty things, and his rivals don't.'

'Do we have time for a little window shopping?' Annie said artlessly. 'Just to make sure everything's up to our standards before we make off with it?'

'Go ahead,' I said generously.

The Secret Stash contained all manner of genuine treasures, the accumulated loot from one man's attempt to acquire all the best toys. I genuinely didn't know where to look for the best. Annie pounced on a copy of Tom Pierce's Grimoire, an eighteenth-century spellbook packed full of transportation spells.

'It does make sense, if you think about it,' I said. 'You didn't really think a single old grey mare could carry that many people to Widdicombe Fair, did you? But a grimoire . . .'

There was a Yeti's foot umbrella stand, a stuffed Grey alien with a very surprised look on its face, and a cocoon big enough to hold a person. It stood upright all on its own, huge and overbearing, staggeringly ugly and disturbingly creepy. Annie walked all the way round it, prodding the lumpy exterior here and there, before finally turning to me.

'What the hell is this?'

'A were-moth,' I said. 'It hasn't finished its transformation yet.'

'What's it doing here?'

'It's all about collectors,' I said patiently. 'People who specialize in this sort of thing go crazy over the rarer variations.'

'What happens when it hatches?'

'The value goes down.'

I looked around the room and rubbed my hands together.

'I think everything here will do very nicely as stock for our new business venture. Goods we can be proud of. All we have to do now is find Tommy Two Way.'

'Gideon,' said Annie. 'Be careful how you break the news to him, about his family. We don't have to be cruel to get him on our side.'

'That's practically our job description,' I said. 'We only hurt the ones who deserve it.'

My compass led us through the mountains of Secret Stash, until finally we emerged into a small clearing, where a grey-headed man with a kind face was sitting patiently in a comfortable armchair. He wore a baggy grey suit that looked as if it hadn't seen a dry cleaner in generations, and he had a cup of tea in one hand and a fat Stephen King paperback in the other. A length of steel chain glowed an eerie green, as it connected his ankle to a heavy steel ring embedded in the concrete floor.

'Hello, Gideon Sable and Annie Anybody!' Tommy said brightly. 'I knew you'd be dropping by today, but I couldn't be sure when. The tides of the Zodiac have been playing merry hell with local causality. I put it down to Venus being in retrograde, the minx.'

I just nodded, as though all of that made perfect sense to me. 'Hello, Tommy. I didn't know you could see the future, as well as teleport?'

Tommy shrugged. 'You can't move things safely through the world like I do unless you can see the true nature of things. Time and Space are linked, though no one ever asked them how they felt about it.'

I looked at him thoughtfully. 'Do you know why we're here?'

'Of course,' said Tommy. 'On the very first day I was brought here, I knew the time and manner of my leaving. You're about to tell me that Honest John arranged the death of my family so that he could have exclusive access to my talent.'

'I have no solid proof of that,' I said carefully. 'No one knows for sure.'

'I know,' said Tommy. 'I've always known.'

'Then why have you stayed here?' said Annie. 'Serving that awful man?'

'Because I knew that doing so would lead to this moment – and Honest John's richly deserved fate. You can free me now, Gideon.'

I took out my time pen and thrust it into one of the glowing steel links. I didn't even have to hit the button; the enchanted chain just exploded. Honest John always did use inferior materials. Annie and I ducked our heads as steel links shot past us, but Tommy sat perfectly still, because he was in just the right place to avoid all of them. When the last of the no-longer-glowing links clattered to the floor, Tommy put his cup and his book down on a handy side table, which I would have sworn wasn't there a moment before, and rose unhurriedly to his feet. He stretched slowly, luxuriating in the freedom of movement, and smiled at me.

'Allow me to repay your kindness by transporting all the amazing things in this room to your new place of business. Somebody had to take over from Harry now he's gone, and I'm glad it's you and Annie.'

I didn't ask how he knew. Sometimes the plan just disappears while you aren't looking, and all you can do is throw up your hands and go with the flow.

'I wish Honest John's Secret Stash was at Old Harry's Place,' said Tommy Two Way.

All the treasures blinked quietly out of existence, without any fuss, and we were suddenly standing in a very large and empty room. Alarms bells immediately started ringing in a cross and frustrated way, like a disturbed and fretful baby. Tommy nodded to me.

'Armed guards are on their way. I would like to stick around and watch what's going to happen, but I have somewhere to be.' He stared off into the distance and smiled at something only he could see. 'I wish I was with my wife and children.'

He disappeared.

'I thought his family was dead?' said Annie.

'They are,' I said.

'Then where has he gone?'

'Best not to think about it,' I said kindly.

The alarms cut off suddenly, as though they felt they'd done all that could reasonably be expected of them, and were replaced by the sound of a great many approaching footsteps.

'Tell me you have a plan to get us out of here,' said Annie.

'Of course,' I said. 'But not yet. It's important that we wait until Honest John gets here.'

Annie stared at me. 'I really don't think he's going to be pleased to see us.'

'We can't just leave,' I said. 'That would be rude. So we'll hang around till he shows his face, and then . . . We can have a nice little conversation – about what he did to us.'

'Revenge is best observed from a distance,' said Annie. 'And preferably well out of range of men with guns.'

I grinned at her. 'Where's the fun in that?'

The door slammed open, and Honest John came storming in, accompanied by a great many men carrying really big guns. Honest John was a short, tubby fellow in a rumpled suit, with a flat, humourless mouth and cold, knowing eyes. He stopped a moment, to glare around at his emptied-out treasure house, and then he fixed his gaze on Annie and me. Some of his security guards started to move forward, targeting us with their guns, but Honest John stopped them with a gesture. He barely spared Annie as Ophelia a glance before giving me his full attention.

'Mad Mental Mickey . . . But who's that in there? Ah, I should have known. Gideon Sable himself, the man with the plan. Which means Ophelia must be Annie Anybody.'

I bowed politely. 'Got it in one.'

'I don't know what makes you think you're going to get away with this,' said Honest John. 'It won't take long to track down what belongs to me, and then I'll just have Tommy bring it all back again.'

'I'm afraid Tommy has left the building,' I said. 'And there's no way you can bring him back from where he's gone.'

Honest John took another look around the empty room, as though still half expecting to see Tommy lurking in a shadow somewhere, and then he shrugged quickly.

'All right, how much is it going to cost me to put this right?'

'More than you've got,' I said.

He shook his head sadly. 'I can't believe you're still holding a grudge, after all these years.'

'You nearly got us killed,' I said.

'You cheated us!' said Annie.

'Why are you taking it so personally?' said Honest John. 'I cheat everyone. People come to me for bargains, not guarantees.' He laughed softly. 'And after all, what did you expect, for what you were paying?'

'I could say something about good faith,' I said. 'But what would be the point?' I fixed him with a steady look. 'You should be careful of the people you cheat when they're on the way down. Because you can be sure they'll remember you on their way back up.'

Honest John shook his head. 'I don't have time for this. I have a business to run and a collection to retrieve. If either of you has a problem with me, take it up with the complaints department.'

'You don't have one,' I said.

'Of course I do,' said Honest John. 'Gentlemen, show them how we deal with complaints.'

All the guards opened fire at once, but I'd had the time pen in my hand even before Honest John entered the warehouse. I hit the button as the guards aimed their guns, and Time crashed to a halt. The light in the room descended into infrared, the roar of the guns was cut off, and the air became thick as treacle. I was careful to take a deep breath before I activated the pen, because there was never anything to breathe in the frozen moment between the tick and tock of the world, and that was enough to make me a little slower off the mark than I'd planned. A cloud of bullets hung motionless on the air, interrupted on their way towards Annie and me.

I moved over to Annie, fighting against the resistance of the frozen world, picked her up and carried her safely out of the line of fire. It was like clutching a statue. I set her down and then headed back to Honest John. Every movement was becoming more of a struggle, but I was still able to drag the man forward, inch by inch, until I had him exactly where I wanted. I forced my way back through the congealed world to stand beside Annie. My head swam madly as my lungs strained desperately for air, but my memories of what that man had done to Annie and me kept me moving. When I was finally in position, I hit the button on the pen and Time crashed back into motion.

The bullets flashed forward, to find Honest John standing where Annie and I had been. They slammed into him again and again, and the sheer impact of so much massed firepower picked Honest John up and threw him backwards. He was dead long before he hit the floor. The security guards saw what they'd done and didn't waste a single moment on recriminations. They just turned and sprinted for the open doorway. They all knew they were out of a job now.

Annie jumped just a little as I appeared beside her, and she realized she wasn't where she had been, but she was used to me messing about with Time. She looked at Honest John's body, lying crumpled and bloody on the concrete floor.

'You killed him,' she said.

'His own people killed him,' I said.

'But you made it happen.'

I nodded. 'He had it coming.'

'Because he cheated us? And so many other people?'

'No,' I said. 'Because he tried to kill you.'

TWO
Would You Like to Buy a Rock?

O ld Harry's Place always made me think of the kind of shop you only find in dreams. Packed full of things you'd spent your whole life looking for and never found. Books that could tell you every secret you'd ever wondered about; photos of the one great love you somehow never met; and maps to all the amazing places you just knew had to be out there somewhere, if only you could get to them. Of course, it's finding such things that lets you know you're dreaming, because life is never that kind.

Still, Old Harry's Place did come amazingly close. Now the shop was under new management, Annie and I were determined to make it that kind of store again.

When we arrived back at the shop, Honest John's Secret Stash was already there waiting for us and taking up most of the floor: a huge heap of strange and wonderful things all piled on top of each other. Annie and I exchanged a look and carefully made our way to the back of the shop to change into our usual clothes. That meant jeans and a T-shirt for Annie (because when she was only being herself, she couldn't be bothered to make an effort) and a black suit with a white shirt for me (because it's a style thing). And then we returned to the mountain of marvellousness, with the light of battle in our eyes, and got stuck in. Wonders and treasures quickly emerged from the pile, to be carefully placed in separate piles, while the occasional item far too commonplace to be inflicted on our customers was thrown over our shoulders and into some shadowy corner.

The really good stuff we immediately put out on display, ready for our Grand Opening. We hadn't decided on a date yet, but the longer the shop remained closed, the more rumours would start to spread that, without Harry, it wasn't worth visiting.

Not entirely to my surprise, it quickly became clear that the interior of the shop was expanding to accommodate all the new merchandise. Walls backed away, the ceiling rose even higher, and shelves and cubicles and display cases appeared conveniently out of nowhere, to provide just the right kind of setting to show off our wares. Annie studied the new or, more properly, old fixtures and fittings, and shot me a look.

'I can't help worrying that we're going to be stuck with one hell of a bill for all these extras.'

'Don't let it get to you,' I said briskly. 'This sort of service comes as standard with Old Harry's Place. I've seen far stranger things happen here, with little or no warning, and Harry never once blinked an eye.'

'I never understood why you spent so much time hanging around here,' said Annie.

I considered several clever answers. In the end, I went with the truth.

'This always felt like home to me. Or what home should have been like.'

'You never talk about your family,' said Annie.

I nodded. 'There's a reason for that.'

'I thought there might be,' said Annie. 'Which is why I never asked.'

'Just as I have never asked why you find it necessary to be so many other people,' I said.

'We appreciate that,' said Annie.

Sometimes the secret of a successful relationship lies in the things you don't say. Because you know the other person would only want to help and would be upset when they found they couldn't. We worked on in silence for a while, sorting and identifying and occasionally pausing to share our delight over a particularly fine piece.

'Maybe that's why Harry decided to leave you the shop,' Annie said finally. 'Because he knew how much it meant to you.'

'He left it to you as well,' I said.

'Only because we're together. Perhaps doing one last good deed for us made him feel like a father figure.'

'That would really be pushing it,' I said.

Annie nodded and went back to work. I took a moment to sit back and take a good look around the shop.

A huge stuffed grizzly bear stood by the front door, ready to act as doorkeeper, security and complaints department. His fur was immaculate, the snarling mouth was packed full of teeth, and the eyes were far too watchful to be glass. I often felt like giving him a good prod here and there, just to check whether he really was stuffed, but given some of the appalling things I'd seen the bear do to people when they acted up in the shop, I had no difficulty in restraining myself. The bear was a bouncer and really didn't give a damn whether you were wearing trainers or not.

I sneaked a look at Annie. She seemed to be happy enough in her work, in her own quiet way. When I first found her, after being separated for so many years, I was shocked at the state of her. The world had beaten her down until there wasn't much left. When she wasn't immersed in the glamour of her other personas, Annie was barely there. She slumped around in the simplest of clothes, kept her hair in a severe buzzcut and hardly made an impression in her own flat.

Since I came back into her life and made her a part of my crew, she had recovered some of her old self-confidence, although I sometimes wondered whether that was because I'd thrown her in the deep end and then dropped a bucketful of piranhas in after her. I watched surreptitiously as Annie bustled cheerfully around the shop, pausing now and again to show off some new prize she'd found. There was dust on the knees of her jeans and smudges on her face, but she didn't seem to mind.

I did my best to catch a glimpse of the old fittings and fixtures as they reappeared, but they seemed to be making a point of always manifesting when I was looking somewhere else. It felt like a game, although I wasn't sure who was playing. I had a sneaking suspicion that while Harry might have departed, the shop still retained some vestige of his personality. I couldn't decide whether I found that comforting or not.

I made myself concentrate on sorting out the treasures from the trash, while still tossing the occasional disappointment over my shoulder. Every good thief needs to be able to tell the difference between the real deal and the merely plausible. Annie looked around as a phoenix egg that wasn't even remotely Fabergé hit the floor with a resounding thud.

'Another dud?'

'Not even close enough to be described as a knock-off,' I said.

Annie shook her head. 'How could someone with Honest John's experience be fooled so often?'

'Because he was always far too willing to accept some expert's opinion,' I said. 'I think sometimes he chose to believe that certain things were real, just so he could tick them off his list.'

Not everything would be going out on display. I had already carried the were-moth's cocoon out to the back of the shop, where it would be safe enough until I could contact some of the more specialized collectors and arrange for a private viewing. I was sure a few new cracks had appeared in the outer casing, and I really didn't want to be around when the death's-head were-moth finally erupted from its cocoon, in all its terrible fury and endless hunger. The ways of the insect world are not ours.

The half-dozen Holy Grails without provenance would have to fight it out among themselves, the steam-powered time machine could wait till yesterday, and the pop-up edition of the Necronomicon was strictly a novelty item. I wasn't sure about Dracula's skull, or the smaller skull of Dracula when he was a boy.

After a while, I took a break, so I could indulge in a long, slow stretch and get my second wind. I looked thoughtfully around at the bare wooden floorboards, and Annie made an impatient noise.

'Are you still hoping to find a hidden trapdoor somewhere?'

'I'm convinced Harry had his own Secret Stash,' I said. 'Locked away, in some carefully concealed cellar.'

'Maybe Harry took the cellar with him when he left,' said Annie.

I had to smile. 'That is the kind of thing he'd do.'

I got to my feet and helped her arrange some of the more interesting pieces on the shelves, although there wasn't as much space as there should have been. Half the shelves were already occupied by items that had somehow hung on from the old shop. Maps of lost lands; medals from wars the history books have never heard of; and a human skeleton with a steel punch hammered through its forehead, tucked away in a hollowed-out grandfather clock leaning casually against the shelves. None of it was particularly valuable, but I was still glad to see such old friends again.

'Why aren't we throwing all of this junk out into the street?' Annie said severely. 'It's just taking up space.'

'Someone might want them,' I said.

'I thought we'd agreed this was going to be an upmarket establishment,' said Annie. 'Not a resting place for the kind of trash Honest John specialized in.'

'Hush,' I said. 'You'll hurt their feelings.'

Annie started to say something and then thought better of it.

'If any of this stuff was actually worth anything, Harry would have taken it with him,' she said finally.

'Perhaps the shop missed having it around,' I said.

Even as I was saying that, long strings of faerie lights suddenly appeared above us, criss-crossing the ceiling in intricate patterns. Wee winged creatures were plugged into every socket, glowing like Christmas decorations.

'What the hell are they?' said Annie. 'And do we need some special kind of spray to get rid of them?'

'They're current junkies,' I said. 'Friendly little things. I think they add a nice festive touch.'

Annie sniffed. 'I can't believe the shop missed them . . .'

'They add character,' I said.

'You say that like it's a good thing,' said Annie. 'Come on, back to work. This treasure trove won't sort itself out.'

'Sometimes I think this place is haunted by the ghosts of merchandise past,' I said, rising unhurriedly to my feet. 'Things that don't want to leave the shop and would only come back again if you sold them. I have to say, I like the idea of items you could sell over and over again. It appeals to my larcenous soul.'

'You'd steal the look in someone's eyes if you could,' said Annie.

I nodded modestly. 'I do love a challenge.'

Some time later, when we were sure we'd broken the back of the work, we sat down together in the middle of the floor. We were both soaked in sweat, and our clothes were thick with dust. I poured us both tall glasses of iced green tea, from a thermos that was never empty and always obliging. There was still work to be done, but at least now the shop was starting to look just a little bit magical again.

'Remember the stacks that used to fill up the furthest reaches of Old Harry's Place?' said Annie. 'All those endless rows, stretching away further than the eye could follow?'

'Of course,' I said. 'Some of them went back so far I was worried I'd end up in Narnia.'

'Do you think they'll show up again as well?'

'Perhaps. When we've got enough stock to justify them.'

Annie shuddered briefly. 'I always felt there should be a sign at the entrance, saying, *Warning! Here Be Tygers!* And what about those back rooms that Harry used to hire out for very private meetings? Where security was so tight that Harry used to boast even God couldn't listen in on what happened there?'

'Given some of the people who used those rooms, that was probably just as well,' I said. 'But every bad penny finds its way home, at Old Harry's Place.'

'We can't keep calling the shop that,' said Annie. 'Not now that Harry's gone. His being here was part of what brought people in, and I can see some of our customers throwing a real wobbly if they pop in and find he's no longer the proprietor.'

'The shop belongs to us now,' I said. 'It should have a name that reflects that. How about Gideon and Annie's Place?'

She gave me a stern look. 'Are we really going to run this place as Gideon Sable and Annie Anybody? Do we want people knowing where they can find us?'

I nodded slowly, acknowledging her point. 'Be sure your crimes will find you out.'

'Perhaps it's time we retired from all that,' said Annie. 'Give up our old professions, and just be shopkeepers.'

It was my turn to give her a stern look. 'We don't just steal from the bad guys for the money and the plunder; we're in it for the adventure. And a chance to stick it to the kind of scumbags who deserve it. We couldn't give that up and still be us.'

'But who is that?' said Annie. 'Given all the people we've been.'

'The man who loves you,' I said. 'And the woman who loves me.'

We shared a smile, but Annie stopped smiling first. She put down her empty glass and looked at me consideringly.

'You know, I have no idea what your real name is.'

I put my glass down, to give me time to think. 'It doesn't matter. I'm not that person any more. I like being Gideon Sable, and I think I've done enough to earn the name and the reputation. But maybe we should be other people while we're running the shop. If only so we can be sure our previous victims won't turn up, banging on the door and demanding their property back.'

'Who do you think we should be?' said Annie.

'I don't know . . . How does Smith and Jones sound?'

'Like we need to think about this some more.' She looked around the shop. 'It is starting to look like something we can be proud of.'

I gestured grandly at the new items set out on our shelves. 'I know some collectors who will howl at the moon and go into their Happy Dance when they see what we have to offer.'

'Are we going to invite some of our old crew to the Grand Reopening?' said Annie.

'That might give the game away if we're planning on being someone else,' I said. 'Besides, the last I heard, the Ghost is still perfectly happy possessing Fredric Hammer's body and doing good deeds with it.'

'Lex and Switch It Sally are still on their extended honeymoon in Paris,' said Annie.

'And no one has heard anything about the Wild Card since he walked behind the curtains of the world and disappeared,' I said. 'In fact, most people seem quite happy about that. Ah . . . that old crew of ours is breaking up.'

'I'm looking for Gideon Sable and Annie Anybody,' said a voice behind us.

Annie and I scrambled quickly to our feet. Standing facing us was a tall figure in an ankle-length trench coat. I looked quickly at the front door and found it was standing ajar. I shot the stuffed grizzly bear a reproachful look, but he avoided my gaze rather than explain how a potentially dangerous visitor had got past him. I fixed my eyes on the new arrival, who stared calmly back at me. A black silk scarf covered the lower part of his face, while the broad brim of his black hat had been pulled down low to hide the rest of it in shadows. All I could see was a pair of icy blue eyes staring unblinkingly back at me.

Our visitor had gone to a lot of trouble to make sure he wouldn't be recognized, but he still had a definite presence, like the prince of some distant realm, travelling incognito. There was also a very real sense of danger to the man, suggesting that only the damnedest of fools would dare try to cross him. I looked to Annie, but she seemed just as thrown as me. I turned back to the newcomer and did my best to channel Harry's casual arrogance and authority.

'I'm Gideon, and this is Annie. Don't get us confused. The shop isn't open yet, and we don't do previews. Who the hell are you, and what do you want?'

'I have something for you to appraise.' The man's voice was deep and sonorous, like a low roll of thunder. 'Something very old and very rare.'

'How did you know we'd be here?' I asked.

'Because it's my job to know things like that,' said the man. 'Do you want to see what I've gone to so much trouble to bring you, or not?'

Annie and I moved closer together, for mutual support. More and more, the newcomer felt like an attack dog on a leash that might or might not hold . . . but I was curious about what he might have. He had to be someone special to have got past the locked door and its defences, which suggested that what he'd brought us might be special, too.

'Do you have a name?' I said.

'Call me Smith.'

I gave him a hard look. That was a standard ploy for anyone who didn't want you to know their real name. A name that meant No Name.

'Is that really the best you can do?' said Annie.

'A rose by any other name would still have thorns,' said Smith. 'And what does a little subterfuge matter to a man with a stolen name and a woman with so many?'

'Get to the point,' I said.

'Of course,' Smith said calmly. 'I have come a long way to present you with something I just know you're going to want to see. A relic from antiquity, a thing of history and legend.'

He brought his left hand out of his coat pocket and showed Annie and me a simple piece of rock, barely large enough to fill his palm. I blinked at it for a moment. It was just grey stone, round and rough, with nothing out of the ordinary about it. And yet . . . the more I looked at the stone, the more it seemed there was something momentous, even significant, about it. As though, just by existing, this small piece of rock weighed down heavily on the world. Despite myself, I took a step forward for a better look. Annie was right there with me.

Smith didn't step back, but he did withdraw his hand a little. To make it clear that while he was happy for Annie and me to look at the rock, he had no intention of handing it over just yet.

'According to ancient legend,' he said, in his deep and measured voice, 'there was once an island where strange bird women called sirens would sing so beautifully that passing ships would be drawn in close, crash against the rocks and drown everyone – because the crews just couldn't stop listening. Until the traveller Odysseus approached this island. He had his crew bind him to the ship's mast and then plug their ears with wax, so they wouldn't be able to hear the song the sirens sang. They passed by the island safely, even though Odysseus begged them to stop; as a result, he became the only person to hear the sirens' song and survive.

'He never told anyone what it sounded like. Perhaps it couldn't be described in words. Down the centuries and all the way up to the present day, the nature of the song the sirens sang has been one of the world's great mysteries. This particular piece of rock is from the island where the sirens lived; it is said to contain the last echoes of their song. Which makes it a very collectible, and very valuable, piece of rock.'

'Where did you get it?' I said.

'From its previous owner.'

'Who was?'

'There are confidentiality issues,' said Smith.

'Lack of provenance will make it difficult for us to establish the stone's true history,' said Annie. 'And that much harder to sell.'

'But you can tell there's something special about it,' said Smith.

'There are all kinds of special,' I said. 'They don't always translate into money.'

And yet the more I looked at the piece of stone, the more it felt as if there was another person in the room with us. The rock had that special presence, like the Maltese Falcon or the last of the Anglo-Saxon Crowns – the kind of prize people would fight and intrigue and die for. I had always made it my business to steer well clear of such dramas until the conflict and bloodshed were at an end, and only then step in to acquire the trophy for myself. But given that just looking at the rock was enough to make me want it, that had to mean other people would want it, too. And pay through the nose for the privilege of owning it.

'Touch it,' said Smith. 'Feel the history and legend stored in a piece of stone.'

I put out my hand, and he dropped the rock on to my palm. It felt surprisingly light, as though it might float away at any moment. Annie reached out a fingertip to touch the thing, and I almost pulled the rock away. All that stopped me from doing that . . . was not being sure whether I was doing it to protect Annie or because I wanted to keep the stone to myself. Something about the rock was speaking to me, and not in a good way.

'What do you think, Gideon?' said Annie.

I kept my voice carefully calm and steady. 'Assuming this is what he says it is, how would we go about confirming that?'

'We need specialists,' she said immediately.

'Like what?' I said. 'A geologist? A historian? Someone who knows all there is to know about ancient bird women girl groups?'

'I used to know a Professor Asutro,' said Annie. 'He specialized in Greek mythology.'

Something in the way she said his name made me want to look at her, but I didn't. Annie didn't mention how she knew him, and I was careful not to press the point. We both have things and people in our pasts that we prefer not to talk about. It was enough for me that she trusted the man's judgement.

I looked up from the stone to ask Smith some more questions, but he was gone. I looked to the front door, and it was closed again. The stuffed bear appeared even more baffled than before. I frowned, as I realized I hadn't heard the man's footsteps leaving, or the front door open and close. And I have always prided myself on knowing what's going on around me. I glared at the bear.

'You are really letting the side down, Yogi.'

The bear had the grace to look a little embarrassed. I hefted the rock in my hand and then turned to Annie, who was shaking her head slowly.

'What is going on here, Gideon?'

'Beats the hell out of me,' I said. 'If this rock really is what Smith says it is, I know collectors who will tear their own hearts out to own it. But I can't believe a lifetime's payout like this would just fall into our hands.'

We both studied the rock carefully. It just sat there on the palm of my hand, doing nothing . . . in an ostentatious sort of way.

'Why would Smith just disappear and leave it with us?' said Annie.

'Because he was scared of it?' I said. 'Or perhaps . . . because we're being set up for something.'

Annie gave me her best *You're being very slow* look.

'Smith might have left it here so he could rush off and tell all the other interested parties that the rock is now in our hands.'

'To make us a target? As in *let's you and him fight*? So he could come back later, after the dust had settled, and all the other claimants had wiped each other out . . . Could be.' I looked at the front door again. 'There are some heavy-duty protections and defences on that door, and Smith walked right through them like they weren't even there. Which would strongly imply he has to be some kind of major player. So why don't I know him?'

'It was a pretty thorough disguise,' said Annie. 'Like you and Mickey – all we saw was the look, not the man inside.'

'If Smith is important,' I said, 'that means there's a good chance the rock is, too.'

'But some valuables are more trouble than they're worth,' said Annie. 'Maybe we'd be better off getting rid of this stony Trojan horse, before some of the more wild-eyed collectors turn up and trash the place.'

My hand closed protectively around the rock. 'Let's not get ahead of ourselves. I want to know exactly what this is before I decide what to do about it. I say we put it somewhere safe until you can contact your professor chum in the morning.'

'Do you think Smith might come back for his rock?' said Annie.

'Let him try,' I said. 'He walked away from it, and I'm not letting it go until I know a lot more about it.'

My gaze moved quickly across the shelves, in search of something I'd put there earlier from Honest John's Secret Stash. I moved over and took down a simple wooden container, with silver hinges and a clasp, covered in long lines of deeply inscribed writing. Annie looked it over carefully and then raised an elegant eyebrow.

'This is the Box Unopenable,' I said, just a bit grandly. 'A hiding place out of legend, where the old priest-kings of Hy-Brasil used to store their greatest secrets.'

'What kind of secrets?' said Annie.

'I don't know,' I said. 'It's a secret.'

Annie gave me a sharp look and then traced a line of the writing with her fingertip. 'What does this say?'

'No one knows,' I said. 'It's the only remaining example of a language forgotten by history. The point is, no one can open this box unless they know the right word.'

'Which is?' said Annie, just a bit pointedly.

I pronounced the word carefully, and the lid rose up on its own. I dropped the rock inside the box, and the lid slammed down, almost taking one of my fingertips with it. I sealed the box again with the word, and then tried the lid, just in case. It remained firmly closed. I nodded, satisfied, and put the box back on the shelf. Annie frowned.

'Shouldn't we at least hide it somewhere?'

'No need,' I said. 'No one else can open it.'

Annie gave me a stern look. 'If you know the word, you can bet good money there are a whole bunch of other major-league thieves out there who also know what it is. Secrets don't tend to last long in our little community.'

'Doesn't work that way,' I said. 'Only the owners of the box can know the word, because it's part of the lost language. And we'll forget it the moment the box leaves our possession.' I yawned and stretched slowly. 'I think we've had enough excitement for one day. Let's shut up shop, go home and get some rest.'

Annie yawned, too, despite herself. 'You've got me started now. Let's go.'

We headed for the front door, and I nodded to the bear. 'Mind the store, Yogi.'

The stuffed grizzly practically bristled with alertness.

Our home was set right at the back of a quiet little cul-de-sac, in a perfectly respectable area, where none of our suburban neighbours had any idea as to who and what we really were. There's nothing like hiding in plain sight.

I parked our nicely anonymous car in our very secure garage, and then Annie and I went inside, leaning companionably on each other. It had been a long and very busy day, so Annie went straight up to bed while I spent some time activating the house's protections and invisible mantraps. When you've made as many enemies as we have, it takes a lot to make you feel secure. I armed the last few exorcism mines and then went upstairs to join Annie.

Not nearly long enough later, a deafening alarm suddenly went off, like all the bells of London crammed into our bedroom. Annie and I sat bolt upright in bed, clutching at each other and staring wildly around. The bells stopped ringing, and it was only then that I realized there was a large stuffed bear standing at the foot of our bed.

'The shop has been burgled!' he growled. 'Get your arses back there right now!'

I gave the bear my best sleep-deprived scowl. 'Yes, thank you, Yogi. Go back and stand guard, until we get there. You can use the time to think up some really good excuses as to how the bad guys were able to get past you twice.'

The bear sniffed sulkily and disappeared.

'That was one hell of a burglar alarm,' said Annie, knuckling at her bleary eyes. 'Did you know the bear could do that?'

'No,' I said. 'Harry always did love his little surprises.'

Annie groaned and pushed back the duvet. 'What time is it?'

I turned on the light and checked the alarm clock. 'Just past three.'

'In the morning?' Annie said loudly. 'Bastards! We never burgled anyone at such an ungodly hour. It's not civilized.' And then she stopped and looked at me. 'Why are you still calling him Yogi? I thought we'd agreed he should be Rupert?'

'I did try,' I said. 'He didn't like it. Besides, he looks like a Yogi.'

I sent our car racing back through London's early morning streets. There wasn't much traffic, most of it transporting goods never dreamed of in daylight. The night people were out and about, steeping themselves in the kinds of sin that can only flourish once the sun has gone down. Some of them recognized us and waved. We arrived at the shop in record time, and I was relieved to find the front door was still closed and that no one had smashed the window. Previously, I wouldn't have

thought such a thing possible, but a lot of strange things had
been happening just recently.

I parked the car right outside the shop, ignoring the parking
restrictions. I didn't bother locking the car; if anyone took it,
I'd just steal a better one. Inside the shop, everything seemed
fine. There was no sign of any damage, all the stock was still
where it should be, and there was no disarray to suggest our
intruder had been searching for something. The current junkies
stirred and murmured resentfully as we looked around, which
suggested our burglar hadn't awakened them. I locked the
front door, to make sure we wouldn't be disturbed, and then
glared at the stuffed bear, but he had nothing to say for himself.

'Something must have happened here,' Annie said quietly.
'To upset Yogi enough to trigger the alarm.'

'I'm not seeing anything,' I said.

'Could Smith have come back?' said Annie.

'The rock . . .' I said.

I went straight to the Box Unopenable, took it down from
the shelf and tried the lid, smiling in relief when it didn't
budge. I spoke the Word, waited impatiently for the lid to rise
and looked inside. At a completely different piece of rock.
Annie saw the expression on my face, crowded in beside me
and pursed her lips unhappily.

'That's not our rock, is it?'

'Different size, different look,' I said. 'And this one doesn't
feel even a little bit special. Someone has taken the important
piece of rock and left us with the booby prize.'

'How could they open the box?' said Annie.

'They couldn't,' I said. 'Nobody could.'

'Then how did they steal the rock?'

'Only one way I can think of.'

I sealed the box again, just in case, and put it back on the
shelf.

'We have to get the rock back,' Annie said firmly. 'If word
gets out that we can be robbed this easily, no one would
have any faith in our security. Thieves would line up to take
a crack at us, and nobody would trust us with their valuables.
What about your compass? Could that point to where the rock
is now?'

I got my compass out and studied it, but the needle wasn't moving. I put it away again.

'The rock's new owner must have surrounded it with industrial-strength protections,' I said. 'That's what I would have done, the moment it was in my hands.'

'Could Tommy Two Way have taken it?' said Annie. 'He got past the shop's protections when he delivered the Secret Stash.'

'He's with his family now,' I said. 'No, there's only one person who could have exchanged the rock for another of similar size, without having to open the box. She wouldn't even have needed to enter the shop.'

'Switch It Sally?' said Annie. 'Why would she rob her friends?'

'Oh, come on,' I said. 'This is Sally we're talking about.'

'She's changed since she married Lex.'

'But what if she didn't *stay* changed?' I said. 'What if the marriage didn't work out, and she's broken up with the Damned?'

'We'd have heard,' said Annie. 'Wouldn't we?'

'We have been very busy,' I said. 'We're going to have to go to Paris, track down Sally and Lex, and see what the situation is. If she has got the rock . . .'

'We get it back,' said Annie. 'Whatever it takes.'

'Damn right,' I said.

THREE
One Man's Rage

'We'll start in Paris,' I said, 'but Sally could be anywhere by now.'

'Are you positive it was Sally?' said Annie.

'Of course,' I said. 'I know her.'

'You used to know her,' said Annie. 'We're not the people we used to be. Why couldn't she have become a better person as well?'

'Because she's Switch It Sally! A hard-headed, hard-hearted thief and confidence trickster, who always put herself first and everyone else nowhere.'

'But she seemed so happy with Lex,' said Annie.

'It's always been a part of Sally's con that she can convince anyone of anything as long as it serves her purpose,' I said.

'You really believe Lex could be fooled that easily?'

'He could if that was what he wanted,' I said. 'If he finally thought he'd found someone who could help him bear the burden of being the Damned . . .'

'But why would Sally want to con Lex?' said Annie. 'It isn't like he's got anything.'

'Sometimes Sally does things just because she can,' I said. 'Or to see if she can get away with it.'

Annie studied me for a moment. 'The way you talk about her . . . What did she do to you, Gideon? Did you let yourself trust her, only to be stabbed in the back?'

'We were never close,' I said. 'We just worked a few jobs together. And, of course, she betrayed me. That's what she does.'

I took out my compass.

'You think you can find Sally with that?' said Annie.

'It always points to what I need,' I said. 'And right now, I need to find Sally.'

'What are you going to do when you find her?' said Annie.

'Take back the rock,' I said. 'And then ask her some very pointed questions.'

Annie smiled. 'So you do care why she did it.'

'I know why,' I said. 'I just need to hear her say it.'

I held the compass out before me, but the needle just spun round and round, unable to settle.

'What does that mean?' said Annie.

'Someone must have placed some really powerful shields around her,' I said.

'So Sally taking the rock could have been someone else's idea?'

I frowned as I thought about it. 'Things have been happening very quickly. First, someone wanted us to have the rock. Then someone else didn't want us to have it. If the rock really is what it's supposed to be, some very determined collector could have reached out to Sally, as the only thief who could steal it for him.'

'Any names you feel like putting in the frame?' said Annie.

I shrugged. 'Too many to choose from. Well . . . if the compass can't find Sally, let's see how it does with the Damned.'

'Are we sure we want to disturb Lex?' said Annie. 'If he and Sally have broken up, he's not going to be in the best of moods.'

'We need to know what's happened,' I said flatly. 'It's always possible they could be working together on this.'

'Why would Lex turn against us?' said Annie. 'After everything we've been through together?'

I met her gaze steadily. 'A man will do anything if the woman he loves tells him to.'

Annie shook her head. 'No. Not Lex. I can't believe that.'

'I can,' I said.

'And if they're not partners, and they have broken up?'

'Then we're going to need the Damned's strength to take down whoever's behind all of this,' I said.

'Would Lex work with us, against Sally?'

'Depends on how bad the breakup was,' I said. 'Hell hath no fury like a lover scorned.'

But when I held the compass out again, the needle didn't move at all. I gave the thing a good shake, but the needle refused to budge.

'Maybe it's broken,' Annie said helpfully.

'More likely, Lex has put his armour on,' I said. 'Spiritual armour made from the halos of murdered angels is enough to hide a man from anything.'

I put the compass back in my pocket and stood for a moment, scowling around the shop as I gave the matter some thought. Despite everything I'd said, I didn't want Sally to be the thief. I really thought she'd changed. But the more I thought about it, the angrier I grew at myself for being so trusting. I should have known better. The leopard doesn't change its spots because it can't. After a while, Annie cleared her throat.

'So,' she said encouragingly, 'what are we going to do first?'

'There are any number of people I could ask, who've been able to find things and people for me in the past,' I said. 'But this is an unusual situation. We don't know why the rock was left with us, or why it had to be taken away from us in such a hurry, and, most importantly, we don't know whether we might be going up against the Damned as well as Switch It Sally.'

'That's a lot of things we don't know,' said Annie.

'So we need someone who does,' I said. 'I know someone who should know, because she knows everything. Or at least she says she does, and I have good reason to believe her.'

'OK . . .' said Annie. 'Who are we talking about? And if she's that useful, why have you never mentioned her before?'

I looked steadily at Annie. 'I need you to be cool and not at all judgemental about who I'm going to have to bring in to help us.'

Annie raised an eyebrow. 'Aren't I always?'

'This is different,' I said. 'Even allowing for some of the weird and wonderful types we've had occasion to deal with, this is jumping over the edge without a parachute.'

'All right,' said Annie, 'I'm intrigued. Who is this woman you have in mind, and what's so special about her?'

I took a moment, so I could choose my words carefully. 'Not everyone I know is, strictly speaking, real.'

Annie frowned. 'Like the Wild Card?'

'No,' I said. 'Johnny Wilde was real; he just didn't pay any attention to the rules of reality, so they tended to look the other way where he was concerned. Sandra Ransom is . . . more complicated. Some say she's the manifested alter ego of a young man who's spent the last several years in a coma after crashing his motorbike. Others say she's the fictional creation of an author who committed suicide but used his last dying energies to bring her to life. Some say she comes from the reality above this one, or the one beneath it. There are a lot of stories about Sandra Ransom, because no one really knows anything.'

'Like Harry?' said Annie.

'Only more so. All I can tell you for certain is that Sandra knows the answers to all questions. As long as you can persuade her to tell you what she knows, and not annoy her so much in the process that she'll turn you into a small green hopping thing with haemorrhoids.'

'Ouch,' said Annie. 'So, what's the best way to persuade her? Bribes, chocolates, promises?'

'All of that helps,' I said. 'But the best way is to get her to like you. Sandra will do anything for you if she likes you – and she'll do anything *to* you if you get on her nerves. It's always a delicate balancing act because you can never tell what might set her off.'

'So, basically, you're going to have to charm her?' said Annie.

'Basically, yes.'

'OK,' said Annie. 'Is there anyone else we could ask?'

'No,' I said. 'We can't contact Sandra directly, because no one can find her unless she wants them to. I know people who can see the past and the future, who could tell you what angels and demons are getting up to right now, and even they couldn't find her. All we can do is reach out and hope she'll come to us.'

'How do we do that?'

'Extremely cautiously,' I said. 'Now, I need you to listen to me carefully, Annie. Once Sandra arrives, you're going to have to be very quiet and let me play this as I see best. You're going to want to help, but you really mustn't. For your own sake. And if I get the sense things are starting to go wrong . . . when I say run, you run. And don't stop to look back.'

Annie looked me in the eye and saw I meant it. That I was genuinely scared of what could happen to her. She nodded reluctantly.

'I understand.'

'No, you don't,' I said. 'Nobody does.'

Annie shook her head impatiently. 'Give me a break, Gideon! What exactly are we talking about here?'

'Some say . . . God's little sister.'

Annie started to say something . . . and then didn't.

I gestured for her to stay put and went to the rear of the store. I came back wheeling a tall standing mirror on squeaky casters.

'Oh no,' said Annie. 'Not him.'

'Hush,' I said. 'You'll hurt his feelings.'

I set the mirror in place before us. It was a good seven feet tall and three feet wide, in a polished cedarwood surround. The reflection didn't show me or Annie, just wispy clouds drifting for ever across an infinite sky.

'He's dreaming,' I said.

The mirror started snoring, like a saw rasping through thick wood. I slapped the top of the mirror's frame.

'Sidney! Rise and shine! Time to earn your keep!'

The snoring broke off abruptly, and the mirror's reflection suddenly showed Annie and me – only not as we were. Instead, I was a sleazy overweight Pierrot, complete with hunchback, while Annie was a slutty Columbine, her face covered in enough makeup to scare off a clown at midnight. We were dancing the Tango. Parading up and down, cheek to cheek, with long-stemmed roses gripped in our teeth, while hot Latin American music blasted out of the mirror.

Annie folded her arms and stared sternly at the mirror. 'Have you been having fantasies about us again, Sidney? Am I going to have to scrub you down with carbolic soap?'

'What do you want?' the mirror said loudly. 'I'm busy!'

Annie hesitated, caught off guard. 'What do you mean, busy? Doing what?'

The music shut down, so the mirror could sniff haughtily at us. Our warped reflections disappeared, replaced by a view of Stonehenge bathed in shimmering moonlight. Little green goblins were rioting all over the stones, as if they were one big adventure playground. The mirror was standing proudly in the middle of the henge, and all the goblins bowed their heads to it in passing.

'What has this got to do with anything?' said Annie.

'Wouldn't you like to know?' the mirror said smugly.

'Sidney,' I said sternly, 'playtime is over. You know I wouldn't bother you unless it was important.'

'That's what you always say,' said Sidney.

'I need your help.'

There must have been something in my voice, because Stonehenge and the goblins disappeared, and for the first time the mirror showed an honest reflection of Annie and me. I hadn't realized how worried I was looking. The mirror sighed heavily.

'Things must have come to a pretty pass if you're relying on me to save the day. All right, what do you need?'

'I need to contact Sandra Ransom.'

The mirror was quiet for a long moment. 'You go right ahead and do that,' he said finally. 'And I will go and hide under my bed and not come out again until it's a whole different century.'

'Come on, Sidney,' I said. 'You're not scared of her, are you?'

'Of course I'm scared of her!' the mirror said loudly. 'That's how you can tell I'm still sane! No one wants to attract Sandra Ransom's attention if they know what's good for them.'

'Why not?' said Annie.

'Because she does good things to people!' said Sidney. 'On purpose. Whether they want her to or not.'

'Do you know what she really is?' said Annie.

'I'm not convinced she is real,' said the mirror. 'It's entirely possible that what she lets people see is nothing more than a comforting illusion, designed to conceal the awful truth. So we won't go mad with fear and horror when we meet her. Some people say she's God's human face.'

'If she was God, I wouldn't need you to contact her,' I said. 'I could just send up a prayer.'

'Sandra is worse than God,' the mirror said grimly. 'She actually turns up in person to answer your prayers. Why do you have to bring me in on this, Gideon? Why not try the Supernatural Exchange; they've got everybody's number. Or there's always the Mediums Message Board; they're probably waiting for you to get in touch. Or you could try sacrificing an imaginary animal; that would get her attention.'

'We don't have time for the usual ways,' I said. 'This is urgent, Sidney. There's a problem with Switch It Sally and the Damned.'

'Are they back from their honeymoon?' the mirror said brightly. 'Did they bring me a present? I love getting presents!'

'What use does a mirror have for presents?' said Annie.

'It's the thought that counts!'

'Just reach out to Sandra Ransom, Sidney,' I said, doing my best to sound calm and casual. 'Tell her Gideon Sable needs to talk to her. Urgently.'

The mirror remained silent for a long moment. When he finally spoke, his voice was low and resigned.

'You are going to owe me big time for this.'

'Sidney . . .' said Annie. 'If Sandra Ransom is so good at staying off everyone's radar, how are you going to find her?'

'Here is wisdom, for those with the strength to bear it,' said the mirror. 'One of the great hidden truths of this reality is that any mirror is every mirror. I can see out of, and hear through, all the other mirrors in the world.'

'All of them at once?' said Annie.

'I am large, I contain multitudes,' Sidney said grandly. 'And I can multitask like you wouldn't believe. Wherever Sandra is currently inflicting herself on the world, I will be able to see or hear or feel her presence. And I'll call out to her. But, Gideon, all I can do is pass on the message. What she does about it is up to her.'

'Understood,' I said.

'And if Sandra should decide to turn up here,' said the mirror, 'let it be very much understood that you are entirely on your own. Just wheel me into the shadows and pretend I'm not here. There are powers and forces at work in this world that no one should mess with, because they are not *of* this world.'

'You actually believe that?' said Annie.

'The trouble is, Sandra believes it,' Sidney said darkly.

Annie looked at me, and I shrugged.

'First rule of the con: nothing is ever what it seems. It could be that Sandra just plays the game better than anyone else. Get on with it, Sidney.'

'This can only go well,' said the mirror.

The reflection went blank as Sidney concentrated, and then a slow, steady darkness filled his frame: a night without stars or end. I caught brief glimpses of massive shapes moving, deep in the darkness, like whales at the bottom of the ocean. And then I saw a human shape, existing where nothing could exist. Sandra Ransom walked steadily out of the darkness and right up to the other side of the mirror: a tall blonde in a long white dress, with bare arms and feet. She had perfect classical features, green eyes, a generous mouth – all the stylized elegance of a Greek statue come to life. She stepped lightly through the mirror and into the shop, then smiled at us easily.

Up close, she had none of the little imperfections that made beauty bearable. Her presence dominated the room and made me feel as though I should drop to my knees and worship her. But I didn't. Because I don't do that. And because I needed her to respect me. All the while, an invisible choir sang loud Hosannahs, while white rose petals fell out of nowhere. Sandra looked up.

'Knock it off. Don't make me have to come up there.'

The Hosannahs fell silent, and the rose petals disappeared. The standing mirror made loud retching noises.

'You could have washed your feet before you walked through me!'

'Hush, Sidney,' said Sandra. 'Working.'

She smiled at me, and it was like being hit in the face by a bucketful of beauty. I made a point of being not at all impressed or intimidated.

'Hello, Sandra. Thanks for dropping by. I could use a little help.'

'That's what I'm here for, Gideon.'

Her voice was completely ordinary. Light, pleasant, just one of us. But I wasn't fooled. I could feel the effort that went into it. She hit me with her smile again.

'It's been a while, Gideon. Why do you only ever call me when you need something?'

'Because you always insist on doing something for me.'

'Is that such a bad thing?'

'I already owe you far more than is good for me.'

Sandra shrugged. 'Only because you choose to.'

'You've done a lot for me,' I said. 'I haven't forgotten it was you who originally pointed me in the right direction to become Gideon Sable.'

'I thought somebody should be,' said Sandra. 'And since I knew for a fact that he wouldn't be coming back, I could see you doing very well in the role.' She grinned mischievously. 'I told you that you'd have fun being him.'

'What did happen to the original Gideon Sable?' said Annie.

'He trusted the wrong woman,' said Sandra. 'And now he's happy for ever. Keep the noise down, Little Miss Who Am I Today? Grown-ups talking.'

I winced; you don't talk to Annie Anybody like that. I shot her a quick warning glance, but she just folded her arms and stared coldly at Sandra. I took a step forward, to draw Sandra's attention back to me. And that was when I realized she was now wearing a white three-piece business suit, with glowing white brogues. Like a power businesswoman come straight from brunch in the Elysian Fields.

'I need to know what's happening with Lex Talon and Switch It Sally,' I said bluntly. 'It's urgent.'

'Isn't it always?' said Sandra. 'Usual terms?'

'Yes,' I said.

'My, you must be desperate,' said Sandra. 'Very well, then. Just for you. Our sweet but somewhat unlikely couple are no longer honeymooning in Paris. Sally has been kidnapped and put to work by a figure in the shadows. She is currently being held . . . somewhere I can't see. Which is strange. We must be talking about someone really powerful, but not one of the usual unusual suspects. Because I always make it a point to know exactly what's bothering their devious little minds, and none of them have been misbehaving recently.'

She shot me a confidential look. 'Sometimes I encourage them to act up a little, just so I can have the fun of slapping them down again. It's a game we play. But now . . . It would appear we have a new player on the scene! How exciting!'

Her outfit changed again: to a white leather military uniform, complete with tall boots and a peaked officer's cap. She looked as if she was anticipating trouble and savouring the prospect of doing something extreme about it.

'What can you tell me about Lex?' I said.

'The Damned has left a trail of blood and destruction all across Europe, searching for his missing wife,' said Sandra. 'Most of the supernatural community has bolted for the hills, pulled up the drawbridge or gone to ground, because Lex has made it known he will kill anyone who stands between him and whoever has taken Sally.'

Bloodstains started to appear on the white leather uniform. Thick drops of blood fell from Sandra's fingertips. The light in the shop slowly darkened, as though a terrible storm was gathering. I was careful to keep my voice easy and unaffected.

'Can you tell me where Lex is? Right now?'

'Of course. He's in London's West End, cutting a bloody path through the Murder Bureau. That delightful little clearing house, where all the best professional killers go to look for work. Lex is currently showing them the real meaning of death and horror. I do so enjoy it when he lets his dark side run free. That man has a real talent for mass slaughter.'

Annie couldn't stay quiet any longer. 'But if Lex has gone to the Murder Bureau, that means he's facing an army of the most dangerous killers in London!'

'In the world, dear,' Sandra said happily. 'But not for much longer. Once Lex takes on his aspect as the Damned, nothing can stand against him, or even slow him down. One of these days, he's going to work out what he really is, and then there'll be trouble.'

She laughed softly, her eyes far away, fixed on something

I was glad I couldn't see. Her gaze snapped back into focus, and she shot me a knowing look.

'I'd get there quickly if I were you. Because once Lex has killed everyone in the Murder Bureau, he won't have any more reason to hang around.'

'Thanks for the help,' I said steadily. 'We can take it from here.'

But Sandra showed no signs of leaving. She was still smiling at me, and it was a cold and terrible thing to see. I struggled to keep my voice steady.

'How are things? Still travelling the world, doing good things to people?'

'Somebody has to,' said Sandra. She fixed me with a level look. 'If you need me, feel free to call on me at any time.'

Something in the way she said that made me pay attention.

'Have you been looking into the future again?'

'I see everything,' said Sandra. 'So be good, for goodness' sake.'

She turned abruptly and walked into the mirror, back to where she'd come from. Her image soon faded away, but she left a trail of bloody footprints behind her on the other side of the glass. Sidney made loud throat-clearing noises and then spat a quart of blood on to the floor in front of him.

'I'm going to reek of blood and leather and Chanel Number Five for weeks! I hate it when she uses me as a doorway. Is there anything scarier than good so pure it's never even heard of mercy?'

'Are you hurt?' I said. 'I mean, damaged?'

'I'll survive. Check your girlfriend.'

I turned quickly to Annie, who was looking seriously pale. She managed a fragile smile for me.

'You weren't kidding about Sandra Ransom. That is one seriously scary lady.'

'Thanks for not getting involved in the conversation,' I said. 'I needed her to stay focused on me, so I could be sure I'd be the only one who'd have to pay her price.'

'It was all I could do to stand my ground,' said Annie. 'It was like one of the ancient goddesses had come down from Olympus to condescend to us.'

'And that was her in a good mood.'

Annie looked at me carefully. 'What is this price you'll have to pay for her help?'

'One day, Sandra will want me to do something for her,' I said. 'Something I really won't want to do. And I will do it, even though it'll probably cost me everything I care about. Because the alternatives would be worse.'

'Couldn't you offer her something else instead?' said Annie. 'We do have all kinds of amazing things in this shop.'

'Sandra doesn't care about things,' I said.

'What would happen if you refused to go along?'

'Remember the small green hoppity things that wince when they bounce?'

Annie looked at me. 'That's a thing? An actual thing?'

'Oh, yes. Trust me, she's done a lot worse in her time.'

Annie scowled. 'I am now changing the subject, because we're a bit pressed for time. But we will come back to this.'

'Looking forward to it immensely.'

'The Murder Bureau,' said Annie, not actually pulling a face but sounding as though she wanted to. 'Of all the places Lex could have gone, he chose to go there? A whole building packed full of hard-core professional murderers, ready to open fire on anyone who even looks at them in a funny way?'

'But like the lady said, not for long,' I said. 'All the guns in the world wouldn't be enough to stop the Damned. He'll kill every single one of them.'

'But why would he even want to go to a place like that?' said Annie.

'He must believe someone there knows where Sally is,' I said. 'Or, at the very least, who was behind her kidnapping.'

'If Sally has been abducted, that means she could have been acting under duress when she stole from us,' said Annie.

'It's possible,' I said.

'Then we have to help Lex find her and rescue her!'

'I don't think it would be a good idea for us to get in the way while the Damned is on a rampage,' I said carefully.

'Sandra knew what Lex is doing at the Murder Bureau,' said Annie. 'And she thought it was funny . . . Isn't she supposed to be one of the good guys?'

'Sandra believes in justice,' I said. 'And there isn't a drop of forgiveness in her. We should be grateful that mostly she doesn't interfere unless she's asked. If she ever decides to get personally involved in Humanity's business, she'll turn our cities into cemeteries. And dance laughing among the corpses.'

'Then it's a good thing she likes you,' said Annie.

'You think that would stop her?' I said. 'All right, we have to get to the Murder Bureau, but we need a shortcut. Sidney . . .'

'Don't look at me!' said the mirror. 'I am suffering from post-traumatic stress disorder after that close encounter with the Divine Bitch.'

'Careful,' I said. 'She might still be listening.'

'What's she going to do?' said Sidney. 'Turn me into a talking mirror? Look, I've had enough for one day. Just tuck me away in a nice cupboard and leave me to get on with some serious whimpering.'

'Not just yet,' I said. 'Harry once told me you picked up some very useful skills during your wanderings in the mystic East, including how to be a dimensional door. That you know how to let people walk through you, to anywhere else in the world.'

'The bastard!' said Sidney. 'He swore he'd never tell. Oh, very well, I suppose I can find you a way into the Murder Bureau. But are you sure you want to do this? Just stroll uninvited into a building full of the deadliest people on the planet?'

'Unfortunately, yes,' I said.

'Give me a minute, and I'll see what I can do. Opening a door in Space and Time isn't like hailing a cab, you know. Especially when there's the Murder Bureau's protective shields to consider. Once this is all over, I expect you to give my frame a really good polish! And use the expensive beeswax!'

'Bless you, Sidney,' said Annie, patting his frame fondly. 'You're a treasure.'

'Then why don't I have a more prominent position in the shop?' Sidney said immediately. 'Instead of always being stuck out back. I should be out front with the bear, greeting the customers.'

'Well,' I said, thinking quickly, 'we can't risk anyone stealing you.'

'Of course,' said Sidney, immediately mollified. 'You're quite right. What was I thinking? Harry thought so much of me he hardly ever let me out of the back rooms.'

'Harry was a prince among men,' I said solemnly. 'Now, please, concentrate on opening a door into the Murder Bureau.'

'I'm looking, I'm looking . . .'

While we were waiting, I took a look around the shop. The light had returned to normal, and everything seemed peaceful enough. The bear was standing guard at the door, nothing was stirring on the shelves, and the current junkies were sleeping peacefully in the faerie lights. Annie quietly tapped my arm, so she could draw my attention to the mirror. Strange views came and went where the reflection should have been: empty deserts, raging waterfalls, snow-capped mountains.

'Is that Sidney thinking or some kind of screensaver?' Annie said quietly.

'I have no idea.' I cleared my throat. 'Time is a factor, Sidney.'

'Don't rush me,' said the mirror. 'I'm still thinking.'

'What is there to think about?' said Annie.

'If I get this wrong, bits of you will end up scattered all over the building,' said the mirror.

'Take your time,' I said. 'I have complete faith in your abilities.'

'I should think so, too,' said Sidney. 'I used to be somebody, you know. I wasn't always a talking mirror.'

'Who did you used to be?' Annie said politely.

There was a pause.

'I don't want to talk about it,' said Sidney. 'OK, hold it . . . I've found a view of the Murder Bureau. But I don't think you're going to want to see it.'

'Show us,' I said.

The mirror cleared to show the lobby of an expensive office building. Marble floor, stylized furniture, modern art prints on the walls. It would have been a very pleasant setting, but now there were dead bodies all over the lobby, and the floor was soaked in blood and gore. More had been splashed across the walls, and some dripped steadily from stains on the ceiling. Something terrible had passed through and left a trail of butchery behind it. I stepped closer to the mirror, trying to get a better sense of what had happened, and Annie moved reluctantly in beside me.

I could see smashed-in heads, backs that had been broken and arms and legs torn away. Many of the faces were screaming silently. Some of the dead still had guns clutched in their hands, for all the good they had done them. In the distance, I could hear intermittent gunfire and the sounds of men dying horribly.

'We've found Lex,' I said.

'He really is damned,' Annie said quietly. 'We can't go in there, Gideon.'

'We have to talk to Lex,' I said. 'If Sally really has been kidnapped, we're going to need the Damned's help to get her back.'

Annie looked at me. '*If* she was kidnapped?'

'We don't know anything for sure,' I said. 'This is Sally we're talking about. I wouldn't put it past her to play both sides against the middle if there was a big enough payday involved.'

'Just because she's an ex of yours . . .'

'We were never close!'

The mirror cleared his throat loudly, drawing our attention back to the bloody scene in the lobby.

'Before you even think about going in there,' said Sidney, 'you need to see what's happening right now. Because I think the Damned has gone insane.'

Annie and I looked at each other.

'Show us,' I said.

The lobby and its piles of corpses disappeared, replaced by a long corridor filled with the sound of gunfire. The first thing I saw was the Damned in his armour. When he was still just a man, he killed two angels, from Above and Below, and cut the halos off their heads. Most of the time, he wore the halos as silver bands on his wrists, but when he unleashed his fury on the world as the Damned, the halos expanded to cover him from head to toe in a spiritual armour of Light and Dark.

It didn't so much protect him as seal him off from the world. The armour made him unreachable and unstoppable, a pitiless force of death and destruction. The darkness of the armour's left side wasn't just an absence of light; it had a terrible presence all its own. The right side blazed so brightly it was like the sun come down to earth.

Armoured by Heaven and Hell, the Damned went to his killing like a hungry man to a feast.

He strode down the corridor, heading unflinchingly into heavy sustained gunfire from dozens of professional killers. They had barricaded themselves behind piled-up office furniture, but it was clear from the look on their faces that they knew it wasn't going to be enough to stop the Damned. A few emerged from doorways just long enough to open fire, and then ducked back again. The roar of so many guns in such a confined space was painfully loud, but it didn't bother the Damned at all.

He pulled men and women out of the doorways, killed them with contemptuous ease and just kept on going. The killers at the barricade were armed with everything from handguns to automatic weapons, but none of them could stop or even slow the Damned. A few threw grenades and incendiaries, and explosions filled the corridor with smoke and flames, but the Damned walked steadily through all of it, perfectly at home in Hell.

Suddenly, he was at the barricades, tearing the heavy furniture apart with his hands. The killers fell back, still firing their useless guns, and the Damned went after them. Armoured fists rose and fell, smashing in skulls and breaking necks. He tore arms out of their sockets and threw them away. Blood sprayed across his armour, like rose-red garlands. The Damned picked people up and threw them at the walls with such force the plaster cracked and broke, and the bodies fell lifelessly to the floor. The Damned walked over the dying to get to the living.

He asked each killer a question before he killed them. I couldn't hear what he was saying, through the screams and the gunfire, but I could guess what it was. The only thing the Damned wanted to know. *Where is Sally? Where is my wife?*

The killers screamed and died, denying any knowledge right up to the end. Some pleaded for mercy, some tried to make a deal, but it was never enough to save them. The Damned killed them all and tossed their bodies aside to get to the next.

One man thrust his machine pistol right into the Damned's armoured face and opened fire at point-blank range, laughing hysterically. The Damned didn't even flinch. Just punched the man in the face with such strength his armoured fist emerged from the back of the man's head. The Damned pulled his hand free, let the body drop and then stopped and looked around, because he'd run out of people to kill.

An awful hush fell across the corridor, interrupted only by the crackling of flames left here and there by the incendiaries. A few sprinklers had activated, but not enough to make any impression on the Hell the Damned had made. He headed for the stairs to the next floor and didn't glance back once at the carnage and destruction he left behind.

The scene disappeared from the mirror. Annie turned to look at me, her eyes wide with shock.

'He has gone mad.'

'No,' I said. 'This is what he was like when I first found him. A man driven by rage and the need to punish the guilty. Not because he's a good man, but as one last act of defiance against the Hell he knows is waiting for him.'

Annie's face was full of horror. 'And you made someone like that a part of your crew?'

'I had to have some serious muscle if I was going to take on Fredric Hammer and his guards,' I said. 'And I thought it might be good for Lex to be a part of something again. For a while, it worked. I saw him take his first steps out of the dark – at least partly because of Sally. But now she's been taken from him, he's fallen back. To the man who can do anything, because he knows he's damned.'

'Save the philosophical discussion for another time,' said Sidney. 'Holding this connection open isn't easy, you know. If you are going through, you need to go soon!'

I looked at Annie. 'You don't have to do this. You could just stay here, while I go and talk to the Damned.'

'Do you think he's in any state to listen to you?'

'I have to try. I've reached him before, when no one else could.'

Annie shook her head firmly. 'If you're going to try to reason with him, you're going to need me. Seeing us together might remind Lex of him and Sally.'

'I'm not so sure that's a good thing,' I said. 'But I'll take all the help I can get. Do you need to change into someone else before we go?'

'I think I have to be me for this,' said Annie. 'We need to remind Lex of what it was like when he was part of our crew. But if we're going into a building full of heavily armed and seriously scared professional murderers, shouldn't we at least arm ourselves first? There must be weapons somewhere in the shop.'

'Almost certainly,' I said. 'But when you're going up against trained killers, you can't hope to match them gun for gun. That's playing their game, on their ground. It's better if we go in empty-handed. That'll keep us sneaky and on our toes.'

'What if we meet a killer who knows all about sneaky?'

'I still have my time pen,' I said.

'Will you please move your arses!' the mirror said loudly. 'The connection is collapsing!'

The view of the corridor filled the mirror, like a glimpse into Hell, and Annie and I walked into it.

The smell hit me first, like a blow to the face. Blood and death, and the stench of torn-open bodies. Thick smoke and burning furniture. It took me a moment to get my thoughts straight, and when I turned to Annie, her mouth was compressed into a thin line. She nodded jerkily, to show she was coping. I glanced back over my shoulder, but there was no trace of the mirror. We were on our own. I started forward, stepping carefully over the dead bodies and doing my best to avoid the spreading pools of blood. I tried not to look at the faces. They might have been professional hit men and women, but they hadn't deserved to die like this. Annie stuck close beside me.

'He isn't using a weapon,' she said quietly. 'He did all of this with his bare hands.'

'He's angry,' I said. 'Out of his mind with loss and the need to do something. He wants to share his pain.'

'I've never seen anything like this,' said Annie. 'It's a slaughterhouse.'

'If it helps,' I said, 'you can be sure that everyone here has murdered people for money.'

'I don't think it does help,' said Annie. 'Why wouldn't any of these people tell him where Sally is?'

'I don't think they knew.'

'And Lex killed them anyway?'

I nodded. 'For the crime of not knowing when he needed to know.'

'Where do we look for Lex?' said Annie.

I listened carefully, past the crackling of the flames, but couldn't hear any gunfire or screams. I pointed to the stairs.

'The last we saw, he was heading up to the next floor. So we follow him. And hope we can catch up to him before he runs out of victims and leaves.'

The Damned had left a trail of bloody footprints all the way to the top of the steps, and we followed them up. It helped a little, to be leaving the stench of death and horror behind us. I tried to take the lead, so I could shield Annie, but she insisted on sticking beside me. When we finally emerged on to the next floor, there were no more bodies. No more blood splashed across the floor or walls or ceiling. Even the bloody footprints had faded away to nothing.

Doors to offices hung open all the way down the corridor, and I made a point of glancing into each room we passed, but there was never anyone in them. It looked as though everyone who'd been up here had gone down to face the Damned, and none of them had come back. And then I heard someone scream at the end of the corridor. I hurried forward, with Annie so close beside me her shoulder pressed against mine. The scream broke off, replaced by the sound of a man pleading desperately. I finally came to a halt in front of a closed office door. Behind it, I could hear the Damned's victim begging for his life. Annie looked at me, rather than at the door. I reached out to open it and then stopped, as the pleas broke off. It was suddenly very quiet in the corridor. I raised my voice.

'Lex! This is Gideon Sable! I've got Annie with me. We need to talk.'

There was no response. Annie and I glanced at each other. She gestured at the door.

'After you.'

I took out my time pen and gripped it firmly. 'Hold on tight to my arm, so the pen will cover you, too. If I have to use this, we're probably not going to get much warning.'

She grabbed my arm with both hands. I opened the door and pushed it carefully back, and together we went into the office to face what was waiting for us.

There was just the one body in the sumptuously appointed office, and it was lying on the floor beside the desk. It didn't have a head. Lex was sitting behind the desk, holding the severed head in his hands and staring into its eyes.

His armour was gone. He looked just as he had when I first met him, in the abandoned Tube station of Hob's Court. As though he had deliberately gone back to what he used to be, before he came to know Sally and dared to dream he could be just a man again. A huge and brutal figure, with broad shoulders and a barrel chest, Lex was wearing nothing but faded jeans and silver bands that glowed at his wrists. His hairy torso was slick with sweat and blood, his eyes were cold, and his mouth was pursed thoughtfully. As though he was contemplating all the awful things he'd done to get this far and wondering whether he cared.

'Lex,' I said, 'it's me, Gideon. And Annie.'

He slowly lifted his gaze to meet mine. His face might have been chipped out of stone. I wasn't even sure he recognized me. And then he looked at the time pen in my hand and nodded slowly.

'You won't need that.'

'Are you sure?' I said.

'You're not the enemy.'

'Well,' I said, 'that's good to know.'

'Why are you still holding that man's head, Lex?' said Annie.

He smiled briefly. 'This was the man in charge. I was so

sure he'd know something useful. I came all this way, across the bodies of so many men, just for this. A head full of nothing.'

He tossed it to one side, and it rolled all the way across the floor to bump up against the far wall.

I decided we needed a declaration of trust. I put away the time pen and showed Lex my empty hands. Annie's grip tightened on my arm. Lex nodded his acknowledgement of my gesture and sat back in his chair.

'Someone has taken Sally.'

'We know,' I said. 'We're here to help.'

'Why?' said Lex.

'Because we're family, you idiot,' said Annie.

Lex managed another smile, just for a moment. Some of the tension seemed to go out of him.

'There was a time I valued that. It seems so long ago now . . .'

'We're looking for Sally as well,' I said. 'She stole something from our shop.'

'We think someone else is using her,' Annie said quickly.

Lex didn't say anything. His face was empty of any recognizable emotion.

'Did anyone here know where Sally might be?' I said.

'I've been following clues and trails, hints and hopes,' Lex said slowly. 'Never stopping, never resting, trying to beat the truth out of people who might have heard something. But no one could tell me what I needed to know. I ended up here because the Murder Bureau supplied trained professionals to all the big names and secret organizations in the hidden world. I was sure someone in this awful place would know something. It seems I was wrong about that.

'They would have told me if they'd heard anything. Even a rumour. They wouldn't have dared hold anything back, not after all the terrible things I did to them.' He stopped to think about that. 'When I'm in my armour, it's like the world is made of paper, and all the people in it are no more than smoke and shadows. I can do anything, because no one can stop me.'

He nodded at the headless body on the floor. 'Twenty-seven confirmed kills of his own, and responsible for God knows how many more. He offered me work once. He didn't try that again after what I did to his messenger.'

'Did you have to kill all those people, Lex?' said Annie.

'There wasn't a single person in this building who didn't deserve what happened to them,' said Lex. 'And I did what I did because I need the word to get out. I want everyone to know exactly what I'm capable of. So they'll know better than to lie to me or get in my way. Most of all . . . I want whoever took Sally to know, so they won't dare hurt her. I'm doing this to keep her safe.'

'And because it makes you feel better,' I said.

He looked at me, and I wondered if I'd pushed him too far. And then he smiled and nodded.

'It helps. But not as much as I'd hoped.'

'I thought you'd mellowed,' I said. 'Particularly after you talked with the rogue angel, Ethel.'

'I did improve,' said Lex. 'But most of that was down to Sally. We were so happy together. She helped me remember what it felt like to be just a man. She even had me convinced I might not inevitably be damned, after all. That I could still be forgiven. I even dared to hope we might have a future together. I should have known better. Because if I wasn't damned before, I am now.'

He smiled again, and it was a cold and terrible thing to see.

'I don't care. I will do whatever is necessary to find and rescue Sally. I will slaughter the innocent along with the guilty and bathe the world in blood if that is what it takes. It's not what Sally would want, but I will do it anyway. And I will never feel sorry for any of it.'

'Lex,' I said, choosing my words carefully, 'this isn't a problem you can solve with brute force. That's why Annie and I came here, to help you. Let us help, and we can charm or con the truth out of people, until we find out who's behind all of this. Once we know who, we'll know where to look for Sally. You need to be part of the crew again, so that when we discover where Sally is being held, we can all sneak in and steal her back. Because that's what we do. If you go in on your own . . . you could get Sally killed.'

I waited, watching closely as he thought it through. Finally, he nodded.

'You could be right.'

I didn't sigh heavily and relax, but I really wanted to.

'Can you tell us how Sally was taken?' said Annie.

Lex settled back in his chair, his eyes fixed on yesterday as though it was years ago. Back when he was happy and the world made sense.

'I left Sally alone in our hotel suite, so I could walk down the street and pick up some more of those pastries she liked. I wasn't worried; no one knew who we really were, and, anyway, Sally could look after herself. When I got back, she was gone.

'I thought I would go out of my mind, not knowing where she was or what might be happening to her. I searched the suite for clues, but all I found was a note the kidnappers left for me. No ransom demand, no threats; just a single line: *She belongs to me now.* That gave me purpose again. To go after Sally and get her back, and kill everyone who'd dared to lay a hand on her.'

'Could this be someone getting back at you for things you've done in the past?' I said.

'If this had been about me, they would have killed Sally and left her body for me to find,' said Lex. 'No, somebody had a use for her. Now you tell me she used her gift to steal from your shop. So as long as she stays useful, she should be safe.'

'Sally's smart,' said Annie. 'She won't have any trouble convincing whoever's got her how valuable she could be to him.'

And I thought but didn't say, *Assuming she needs to . . .*

'What did she steal from you?' said Lex. 'Was it valuable?'

'We think so,' said Annie.

He didn't take his eyes off me. 'Then Sally could have been taken just so she could use her gift to steal from you. Which makes it your fault she was kidnapped.'

'You know better than that,' I said steadily.

He nodded. 'You can take your hand off the time pen, Gideon. It wouldn't have any effect on my armour anyway.'

I took my hand back out of my jacket. 'There's nothing more you can do here, Lex. Come with us. I think I know someone who might be able to point us in Sally's direction.'

'But if Sandra Ransom didn't know . . .' said Annie.

Lex looked at me sharply. 'You talked to her? Even I have more sense than to mess with that one.'

'Sandra and I go way back,' I said. 'And she doesn't know everything. She just likes to give that impression. So, when brute force won't work, go with the sneaky.' I grinned at Annie. 'Remember Madam Osiris?'

'Oh no,' said Annie. 'Not her.' She stopped and looked at me. 'What made you think of her?'

'I don't know,' I said. 'The name just popped into my head. What matters is that she knows things.'

Lex frowned. 'I don't know the name.'

'Really?' I said. 'She knows you.'

I remembered Osiris making me promise that I would do whatever it took to protect her from the wrath of the Damned. Did she know this day would come? And what could she have done, or be going to do, to make such a promise necessary? I shrugged mentally and raised my voice.

'Sidney! Get us out of here!'

The tall mirror bullied itself into existence, standing right next to me. 'What am I, your personal taxi service?'

Lex got to his feet, shaking his head. 'You have the strangest friends, Gideon.'

FOUR
Answers and Questions

We'd only just stepped out of the mirror and into the shop when Annie looked Lex over and shook her head decisively.

'Stand right where you are, Lex. I don't want you dripping blood and gore all over our nice new shop. I've only just got the place cleaned up. Make like a statue, while I go and find you a towel.'

Lex nodded obediently, and Annie bustled off to the rear of the shop. I was quietly amused at the way Lex just went along with Annie and her fussing. He was the Damned, after all, which meant no one could make him do anything he didn't want to. I had the good sense to keep that thought out of my face while Lex looked around the shop. He took in the new stock, raised an eyebrow at the current junkies snoring quietly overhead, nodded familiarly to the bear by the door, and only then turned his attention to me.

'Looking good, Gideon. Quality merchandise and an enviable range. If I had any money, I'd certainly spend it here. You'd hardly know Harry had left.'

'That is the idea,' I said. 'Carrying on the grand old tradition of magic for sale – at almost reasonable prices.'

'What did Sally steal from you?' said Lex.

'A piece of rock,' I said. 'Supposedly, a very valuable collectible.'

'How badly do you want it back?' said Lex.

'I want the rock and Sally back,' I said carefully. 'That's why we came and found you.'

'Sally comes first,' said Lex.

'Of course,' I said. Because I wasn't stupid. Arguing your corner is for when you're dealing with sane people.

'So!' Sidney said suddenly from behind us. 'This is the

legendary Damned. Big, isn't he? And messy. I just know I'm going to stink of blood and sweat and testosterone for ages and ages. Maybe I should have you drive a flock of sheep through me, so their wool could scour me clean.'

Lex turned unhurriedly to consider the talking mirror. He took a moment to study his reflection, and the mirror had enough sense to show the Damned as he was, with no embellishments. Lex nodded slowly, looked back at me and raised an eyebrow.

'One of Harry's old toys?'

'I am not a toy!' Sidney said fiercely. 'I am a mirror on the world and everything in it. I see all, and don't you forget it!'

Lex was very nearly smiling. 'Loud, isn't he?'

'You have no idea,' I said.

Lex turned back to face the mirror, and it actually flinched under the impact of the Damned's gaze.

'If you see all,' said Lex, 'can you see where Switch It Sally is, right now?'

'Not as such,' said Sidney, in a somewhat politer tone. 'She is currently hidden away behind the kind of impenetrable shields and protections that would give God a headache. But once Gideon has pinned down Sally's current location, I can take you right to her. Which makes me your best friend, Damned Boy, so you'd better treat me kindly!'

'I don't have friends,' said Lex.

'What about me and Annie?' I said.

He glanced at me briefly. 'You're not friends. You're family.'

Annie came bustling back with a bucket of water, soap and flannel, a scrubbing brush, and a towel draped over her shoulder. She was also pushing a travelling rail of assorted suits ahead of her. She'd been busy.

'Clean yourself up, Lex,' Annie said briskly. 'Before our air conditioning commits suicide. And make sure you use the scrubbing brush to reach those important little places. Once the blood dries, you'll have a hell of a job getting it out of your crevices.'

'I have had to deal with blood before,' said Lex.

'Doesn't surprise me in the least,' said Annie. 'Now get on with it, before I have to go and stand downwind. You whiff like a slaughterhouse where all the guys with hammers are on overtime.'

Lex looked at me. 'Is she like this at home?'

'I'll never tell,' I said.

'Strip off those jeans and start scrubbing,' said Annie. 'Before I get the bear to come over and help you.'

Lex set about making himself presentable again. I nodded to Annie and gestured at the rack of suits.

'Where did you find those?'

'Out back. Some of the old storerooms have reappeared.'

I wasn't sure whether that was a good thing or not. Harry's storerooms were famously prone to sudden surprises.

'Don't worry,' said Annie. 'I just grabbed what I needed and backed straight out again. We can check them for deadfalls and mantraps later.'

'This sort of thing should definitely have been mentioned in the lease,' I said.

'We've got a lease?' said Annie.

'I don't see why not,' I said. 'We've got everything else.'

Annie looked over at Lex, who had stripped down to his shorts and was squeezing a blood-soaked flannel into the bucket. Parts of him looked cleaner. Annie shook her head.

'When you're done, Lex, and not one moment before, look through the suits. Any of them should fit. I have a lot of experience when it comes to clothes.'

'Weird eye for the damned guy,' I said.

They both looked at me.

'Sorry,' I said.

'Why do I need a suit?' Lex said mildly. 'Are we going somewhere formal?'

'I've seen some of the things you wear by choice,' said Annie. 'I am not going anywhere with you looking like a refugee from a low-budget horror movie. Just dump those jeans in the bucket when you're through; I'll dispose of them later. When I can find a pair of tongs long enough to handle them with.'

'Those are my favourite jeans,' said Lex.

'I'll see if I can salvage them,' said Annie. 'If you're good.'

Lex nodded and attacked his left shoulder with the

scrubbing brush. I took Annie by the arm and led her off to one side, so we could talk privately.

'He's only being reasonable because he needs our help,' I said quietly. 'Don't push him too hard, or he might decide he doesn't need us after all.'

'That bucket already looks like it's full of blood,' said Annie. 'And he stinks of death.'

'Of course he does,' I said. 'He's the Damned.'

'The suits should help.'

'I've always admired your optimism,' I said.

Annie looked at me for a moment and then lowered her voice. 'Do you really think we can get Sally back, alive and unharmed?'

'She's only been gone a while,' I said carefully. 'As long as she's still making herself useful, she should be safe enough. Getting her back . . . depends on who's got her.'

'But if we've got the Damned on our side . . .'

'Lex is a one-man army,' I said. 'But if it comes to a straightforward confrontation, all the kidnapper would have to do is threaten to kill Sally, and we'd have no choice but to back off. We need to sneak up on the situation, and for that we need a plan. But I can't put one together until I have some solid information about Sally and her surroundings.'

Lex's voice rose behind us. 'Well, what do you think?'

I turned to look with a certain sense of foreboding. Annie braced herself. Lex stood stiffly before us, dressed in a smart navy-blue suit topped off with an old school tie. If that came from the back room, I had to wonder where Harry got it. I didn't think demons went to Eton, although I could be wrong. Lex looked to Annie and me for our opinions, and I honestly didn't know what to say. The suit was doing its best, but the Damned still looked like what he was.

'Well?' said Lex. 'How do I look?'

'Civilized,' I said.

'Good disguise,' said Lex. He stretched slowly, and I was sure I heard seams splitting. Lex moved over to look at himself in the mirror, which started to back away until Lex glared at it. He studied his reflection carefully and then nodded.

'Smart.' He turned to fix me with his unblinking gaze. 'You said we needed Madam Osiris. Who is that?'

'Soothsayer, confidence trickster and an expert at thinking around corners,' I said. 'Which is exactly what we're going to need.'

'Can we trust her?' said Lex.

'She'll hold up her end of whatever deal we make,' I said carefully. 'As long as we keep a close eye on her and don't let her anywhere near the family silver.'

'Where is she?' said Lex.

Sidney interrupted me before I could say anything. 'Don't ask me to find Madam bloody Osiris! Just trying to cope with that much weirdness is enough to give me a splitting headache in the head I don't even have any more.'

'Are you saying you can't take us to her?' said Annie.

'I can't even see her!' said Sidney. 'And I can see the dark side of the moon during an eclipse.'

Annie looked at me sharply. 'How could a small-time con artist like Madam Osiris hide herself from Sidney? And how can she help us find Sally, when Sandra the living goddess couldn't?'

'Because Madam Osiris is seriously weird!' Sidney said loudly.

'There's more to Osiris than meets the eye,' I said. 'That does tend to come as standard with most of the people in our line of business, but Osiris is just a bit special. Trust me, she is what we need for this.'

Annie sniffed and folded her arms. 'I'm guessing we shouldn't expect to find her where we last saw her?'

'Osiris never stays in one place for long,' I said. 'She doesn't dare. Far too many people are looking for her, with retribution on their minds. She'll have set herself up in a whole new situation by now. But I'm pretty sure I can track her down.'

I got out my compass, and Annie glared at it.

'You're not going to try that useless object again? I wouldn't trust it to point to the fire exit.'

'Have a little faith,' I said. 'Osiris always leaves a back door open for me.'

'Because you're old friends?' said Annie.

'Because I'm one of the few people who'll still take her calls when she's in trouble.'

I held the compass out before me and concentrated on Madam Osiris. The needle spun round once and then pointed steadily.

'What are we supposed to do now?' said Lex. 'Walk in a straight line until eventually we end up standing in front of her?'

'The compass tells me things,' I said loftily. 'And right now, it's telling me we need to visit Brighton Pier.'

'What's she doing in Brighton?' said Lex.

'Conning somebody,' I said. 'But . . . she won't necessarily look like Madam Osiris any more. Like all good scam artists, she has more than one face to show the world.'

'You mean she can put on other personas, like me?' said Annie.

'Well, not like you,' I said. 'Given the kind of seriously unpleasant people who are always on her trail . . . Osiris tends towards more extreme measures.'

'You are really not selling this person to me,' said Lex. 'Why should I trust Sally's safety to someone who's already on the run from people she's cheated?'

'Trust is probably not the best word to use,' I admitted. 'But I'm sure she'll help us out. Once I've made it clear that it's in her best interests to do so.'

'And just how are you planning to persuade her?' said Lex.

'With a nicely considered mixture of bribes, threats and blatant sentiment,' I said cheerfully. 'I know how to reach what passes for a heart in her withered breast.'

I turned to face the standing mirror, which again interrupted me before I could get a word out.

'Don't bother with appeals to my better nature, because I had it surgically removed and spat on. I'm only prepared to do this because I know that if I don't, you'll just keep pestering me. So . . . line up, line up! The excursion for Brighton Pier starts here. All the fun of the fair, including overpriced side-shows, food so fast it'll be in and out of you before you know it, and games of chance rigged till the odds weep bitter tears. And more seagull poop in one place than you would think possible. But please bear in mind that while I am prepared to take you there, I have no intention of hanging around afterwards. Salt air is very bad for my sciatica. And stay away from the candy floss. It's all chemicals these days.'

'Thank you, Sidney,' I said.

'But this is absolutely my last trip!' said the mirror, doing his best to sound as if he was scowling. 'I need my beauty sleep! Or I'll look terrible in the morning.'

Lex looked at me. 'Have you thought about getting a dog instead? I'm told they make excellent pets.'

'I am not a pet!' said Sidney.

Annie glared at us like a teacher burdened with a pack of unruly children.

'Why are we still standing around? Sally needs rescuing!'

'I hadn't forgotten,' said Lex.

'Come on, Sidney,' I said encouragingly. 'The sooner you drop us off in Brighton, the sooner you can go back to sulking in a corner.'

'I'm too nice, that's my problem,' said the mirror. 'People take advantage of my good nature.'

'I can see how that would be a problem,' said Lex.

The mirror showed us a view of Brighton Pier, packed full of happy holiday crowds, and I led the way through.

It was still early in the morning back in the shop, but when we stepped out of the mirror and on to the pier, the sun was high in the sky, and the sunlight was unrelentingly fierce. The gusting breeze was full of the scent of the sea, and keening gulls wheeled overhead.

We'd arrived at the far end of the pier, with a marvellous view of the ocean meeting the horizon. The waves were full of swimmers enjoying the bracing chill of the waters, and all I could think was *Rather you than me.* Two bronzed youths on jet skies were playing dodgems. I foresaw a lifeboat in their immediate future.

I glanced behind me, but there was no trace of the mirror. All the way down the pier, all I could see were milling crowds of holiday people, grimly intent on having a good time. Dated music blasted out of the overhead speakers, and a huge mechanical clown was laughing like a thing possessed.

'Why is no one reacting to our having appeared out of nowhere?' Annie said quietly.

'Sidney takes care of the details,' I said. 'It's all part of the service.'

'Where did Harry find him?' said Lex.

'You'd have to ask Sidney,' I said, 'although his answer will probably change every time you ask. Harry never said anything, but he always did prefer to keep his secrets close to his chest. Of course, in the mirror's case, that could be down to simple embarrassment.'

'Do you have any idea who Sidney used to be, before he was a mirror?' said Annie.

I had to smile. 'That might or might not turn out to be a true thing. You can't trust everything a mirror says. Especially if he starts going on about which of us is the fairest of all.'

'Where is this Madam Osiris?' said Lex. 'I don't want to be here any longer than I have to.'

'No one will pay you any attention,' I said. 'Not in your nice new suit.'

'The prey can always sense a predator,' said Lex.

'Can't you just take a moment to enjoy yourself?' said Annie. 'Pretend you're on holiday?'

'Not while Sally is still in danger,' said Lex.

'Of course,' said Annie. 'I'm sorry. I forgot for a moment.'

'I can't,' said Lex. 'There isn't a moment when I'm not thinking about what she might be going through. When I get her back, I swear I am never taking my eyes off her again.'

I considered the famous free spirit that was Switch It Sally and thought, *Good luck with that.*

'I'm not seeing Madam Osiris either,' said Annie, peering around at the various stalls and attractions. 'Are you sure she's here?'

'We are exactly where we need to be,' I said.

I pointed to a brightly striped tent, standing off to one side. A large sign at the entrance proclaimed: *Murray the Mentalist! Answers to Your Every Question! Step Inside and Find Out What the Future Has in Store for You!* On the other side of the entrance stood a painted portrait of a man in a smart dinner suit, topped by a black silk turban with a fiercely glowing blood-red jewel. His arms were thrust out in a mystical gesture, in a way that suggested his hands might fly away at any moment.

Basically, he looked like an old-fashioned stage magician, the kind with flags of all nations tucked up his sleeves and concealed doves for every occasion. It wasn't an image that inspired confidence on any level, and I quickly shot my companions my most reassuring smile.

'This is the place!'

'I thought we were looking for Madam Osiris?' said Annie.

'Not as such,' I said.

'Can this Murray tell us where to find her?' said Lex.

'In a manner of speaking,' I said. 'Follow me in, follow my lead, and whatever you do, don't get close enough for him to pick your pockets, because old habits die hard.'

'I don't have anything in my pockets,' said Lex.

'He doesn't know that,' I said.

Lex scowled at the tent flaps. 'I am not wasting my time on some sideshow magician.'

'Trust me,' I said.

Lex growled under his breath. 'You ask a lot sometimes, Gideon.'

'Because I'm worth it.'

I strode into the tent like a detective with a search warrant. Annie moved quickly in after me, and Lex brought up the rear. Inside, we were pretty cramped for space. Annie and I had to press close together, while Lex glared balefully over our shoulders. The light was suitably gloomy and mysterious, courtesy of a single rose-tinted light bulb. The tent walls were bare, and there wasn't even a threadbare carpet to cover the pier's floorboards. The air was lightly scented with exotic spices, although the only one I could identify was cardamon.

Murray the Mentalist was sitting on a folding stool, behind a very basic table with a large crystal ball. Compared to the idealized image on the portrait outside, Murray looked more than a little shabby. His turban was a couple of sizes too small, and the jewel at the front was obviously a fake. He looked undersized for his suit, as though he'd bought it off the rack in a hurry. Shiny white cuffs protruded from his sleeves, large enough to contain a multitude of surprises. His face was puffy, and the goatee beard could have used a trim.

When we came in, he was reading one of the trashier gossip magazines, but he quickly dropped it to the floor when he realized he had customers. He sat up straight, thrust out his long-fingered hands in a dramatic gesture and addressed us in a deep booming voice.

'Welcome to my mystical lair, wherein all the mysteries of the future shall be laid bare . . . Oh, it's you, Gideon. You took your time getting here.'

He slumped back on to his stool, dropped his hands resignedly and let his voice relax into a more everyday tone.

'I've been waiting for you all morning. The stars told me you and your friends would be turning up today, but they've never been very exact when it comes to timing. Hello, Annie, you're looking very yourself. And hello, Lex, damned good to see you. Don't look for somewhere to sit; none of you are staying.'

'Good to see you again,' I said.

Annie frowned at me. 'I don't get it. I thought we came here to talk to Madam Osiris?'

'We are,' I said. 'The gentleman before you used to be Madam Osiris. Though neither of them would qualify as real people, with actual lives and histories.'

'Exactly,' said Murray. 'They're just faces I put on, to suit whichever con I'm running.'

'You mean . . . Madam Osiris was just you, dressed up?' said Annie.

Murray smiled condescendingly. 'Oh, please, nothing so pedestrian. I am a professional. I can manifest as a man or a woman, as necessary. A modern-day Tiresias, shuttling endlessly between the sexes. You would not believe some of the people I've been, down the years. Gideon could tell you a few stories – although if he does, I'll drop an anvil on him. One actor in his time plays many roles . . .'

'He does when he has as many enemies searching for him as you do,' I said.

Murray shrugged easily. 'Well, quite. The point is, I can be whatever people I need to be, to make the con work. And try not to look so disapproving, my dear Annie; always remember that every con is based on the principle that you can't cheat an honest man. Only those with greed and avarice in their souls, looking for an unfair profit or advantage.'

'Let me get this straight,' said Annie. 'You can exist as a man or a woman, just by thinking about it? How does that work?'

Murray scowled. 'Never con a pookah. Those creatures have no sense of humour.'

'Don't ask any more,' I said to Annie. 'The story changes every time he tells it, and it's never an edifying one.'

Lex cleared his throat loudly. 'How is a small-time fake like this going to help us find Sally?'

'Because he's not a fake,' I said. 'He really does have genuine abilities; he just doesn't dare use them most of the time. Isn't that right, Murray?'

He nodded stiffly and then fixed me with a stern look. 'How were you able to find me? When the stars warned me to expect you, I thought they must have got the wrong number. I severed all ties with Madam Osiris before I left London. Nobody should have been able to track me here once I'd changed to Murray. Even my aura is different. No, don't tell me how; I don't want to know. The stars will have their way, the bastards.' He scowled at me. 'You broke the crystal ball Osiris gave you, didn't you?'

'How do you know that?' said Annie.

Murray smiled smugly. 'Didn't you see the sign outside? The clue is in the title. I know what I need to know, when I need to know it. And if you find that confusing, think how I feel. What's inside my head is constantly changing, as the stars insist on updating me. Now what the hell happened to my crystal ball, Gideon?'

'A gorgon looked at it,' I said.

'Ah . . .' said Murray. 'Yes, that would do it. All right, Gideon, let's get down to brass tacks. What do you want from me this time?'

'Don't you know?' I said.

Murray sniffed. 'The stars don't sweat the small stuff.'

'Hold everything,' said Annie, leaning forward for a better

look at Murray's face. 'The last time I saw you, as Madam Osiris, you'd had your eyes removed and replaced with miniature crystal balls! And now they're perfectly normal!'

Murray sighed. 'Do pay attention, dear. That was her, and this is me. We're completely different people.' He glanced reluctantly at Lex. 'Your big friend is looking a bit impatient. And yes, of course I know who and what he is. Lex Talon, the killer of angels, the punisher of the guilty, on the fast track to Hell and trampling everyone else underfoot in his hurry to get there. I understand you've killed an awful lot of people just recently, Lex. Or should that be a lot of awful people? Either way, I'm easy; I'm sure you had good reasons.'

'Flattery will get you nowhere,' said Lex. And then he frowned. 'How do you know what I've been doing?'

'You make a big impression on the world,' said Murray, looking just a little nervous under the pressure of Lex's unblinking gaze. 'You do tend to stand out, in the past and the future. Wherever I looked, there you were.'

'I don't like being spied on,' said Lex.

Murray turned quickly to me. 'Remember, Gideon, you promised Madam Osiris you'd keep us safe from the fury of the Damned.'

'I hadn't forgotten,' I said.

Lex frowned at Murray. 'Why would you need protecting? I don't even know you.'

Murray kept his gaze fixed on me. 'You gave me your word.'

'I won't let him hurt you,' I said. 'Whoever you are.'

'Why would I want to hurt you, little magician?' said Lex. 'What have you done?'

'I know why you're here,' said Murray. 'You want to know who kidnapped Switch It Sally. Well, the order to abduct her came from a collector called Coldheart. He got the name because he only ever cares about the things he accumulates, never people. Sally's safe enough for the moment because she's useful to him. But once Coldheart doesn't need her gift any more, he'll have no reason to keep her.'

'You mean he might just let her go?' said Annie.

'After everything she's seen of his base and his operation?' said Murray. 'No, I really can't see that happening.'

'You think he'll kill her,' said Lex.

'Coldheart,' said Murray. 'The clue is in the name.'

'I don't think we need to worry about that just yet, Lex,' I said quickly. 'Sally will grasp the situation and figure out the best way to make herself useful. She'll buy us the time we need to get to her.'

Lex was still scowling at Murray. 'How do you know all this?'

'Hello!' Murray said loudly. 'Murray the Mentalist! The clue is in the name!'

'No,' said Lex. 'There's more to it than that.'

His brow furrowed dangerously as he thought about it. Annie seized the moment to gesture at the shabby trappings of Murray's tent.

'If you have real powers, why are you here, telling tourists they're going to meet a tall dark stranger and to beware the tides of March?'

'Murray has made a great many enemies down the years,' I said. 'Some of them quite appallingly powerful. As long as he keeps his various heads down, he'll live longer.'

'Exactly,' said Murray. 'The first time I raise my head above the parapet, some supernatural sharpshooter will blow it right off. I am obliged to hide my considerable light under this insignificant bushel until it's finally safe for me to come out and show the world the real me again.'

'You honestly think that's ever going to happen?' I said.

'I'm working on it,' said Murray. 'I have plans. I can always kill off a few of my old selves in a really convincing manner, to throw the bastards off the scent. There's nothing like being dead to stop people looking for you. Some of the old faces were getting a bit dated anyway.'

'Where is Sally, right now?' said Lex.

'She's in America,' Murray said quickly. 'In – or, more properly, under – the city of Seattle. Coldheart is one of the world's most serious specialist collectors, and Sally's gift makes her exactly what Coldheart needs to acquire certain very rare and well-guarded items. He won't want to give her up just yet.'

'How did he find out about her?' I said. 'There aren't many who know what Sally can do.'

Murray took a deep breath and braced himself. 'Because I told Coldheart's people all about Sally and where they could find her.'

Lex started forward, his huge hands clenched into fists. The table and its crystal ball went flying, and Murray jumped up from his seat and backed away until he reached the rear of the tent. I moved quickly forward to place myself between Lex and Murray, and the Damned stopped. I was relieved about that, because my plan didn't have a second part. Lex glared past me at Murray, who immediately raised his voice.

'You promised you'd protect me, Gideon!'

'I know,' I said.

Lex turned to me, and his gaze was dangerously cold. 'Do you really think you can stop me?'

'Think about it, Lex,' I said steadily. 'I'm the one who got you out of that abandoned Tube station and back into the light. I made you part of a crew that brought down the worst man in the world and took on the biggest casino in Vegas. I put you together with Sally. And on top of all that . . . If I need to find a way to stop you, I'm sure I can steal something that will get the job done. But I'm hoping you'll stop this because I'm asking you to.'

'He betrayed Sally,' said Lex. 'He's why she was taken from me.'

'Yes,' I said. 'He did that. Because that's what he does. But I need you to trust me on this, Lex.'

'Trust doesn't come easy to the damned,' said Lex.

'Just as well we're friends, then,' I said. 'Look, this man is our only way of getting to Sally. He knows things. Let him tell us what he knows.'

Lex growled, and it was a dark and dangerous sound. But a little of the tension went out of him, and he nodded slowly to Murray.

'Tell us what you did.'

Murray pulled what was left of his dignity about him but didn't move away from the rear of the tent. His words almost tumbled over each other in their hurry to ward off the Damned's anger with useful information.

'The stars told me that Coldheart had people out looking for

Madam Osiris. So I shut her down and moved here to be me.
I thought I'd dynamited all my bridges behind me, but the very
first day I set up on the pier, two of Coldheart's people came
barging into my tent. They told me I could cooperate or die; it
was up to me. And I believed them. We are talking very well-
known, very dangerous people. Cleopatra Bones, who's killed
at least one man with every kind of weapon there is. And her
husband, a Mime Called Malice, who can make a physical
object out of anything he mimes and use it to kill you.

'Cleopatra told me that Coldheart was looking for a thief
with a particular skill set. Either I helped them find one or
they would take turns killing me in slow and horrible ways.
And I believed her! So I gave them Switch It Sally.'

'How did you know where to send them?' said Lex.

Murray just looked at him. 'Oh, come on! When word got
out that the Damned had got married and was on his honeymoon in Paris, the supernatural scene went mad with gossip!
Look, it was either Sally or me, and she had you to protect
her. How was I to know you'd go off and leave her on her
own?'

Lex started forward again, but I was still there to block his
way. For a moment, we stood face to face, but I didn't budge
an inch. When all you have is your reputation, you have to be
ready to defend it. Lex glared past me at Murray.

'You told Coldheart's paid killers where to find Sally?'

'Yes,' said Murray. 'And that's why I'm still here.'

'Not for long,' said Lex.

He put a hand on my shoulder to push me out of the way,
and I held up my time pen. Lex stopped and looked at it
thoughtfully. I remembered him saying the pen couldn't affect
him in his armour, but that was just his opinion. I wasn't sure
myself, but I acted as though I was.

'I can freeze you in Time,' I said. 'Wrap you in the tent,
throw you over the side of the pier and leave you to walk back
to shore. Madam Osiris made it possible for us to crack the
casino in Vegas, where you married Sally. So you could say
you owe that to the man in front of you.'

I looked carefully at Lex to see if my words were having
any effect, but his face was unreadable.

'Please don't hurt him,' I said. 'We need him.'

'I can tell you exactly where to find Sally,' said Murray, his voice full of the knowledge that he was fighting for his life. 'But I can't tell you how long you have before Coldheart decides he doesn't need her any more.'

'Tell us how to save her,' said Lex. 'And save yourself.'

Murray nodded quickly. 'Well, that sounds eminently reasonable.'

Lex turned his gaze to me. 'Don't ever threaten me again, Gideon.'

I smiled easily back at him. 'It's my crew, Lex. I run things because I'm the man with the plan, and the only one who sees the big picture. You're strong, but I'm sneaky. And I have more tricks up my sleeve than you ever dreamed of.'

Annie eased forward to stand beside me. 'We're your friends, Lex. We're Sally's friends. We'll do whatever it takes to get her back safely.'

Lex looked at her for the first time. 'Whatever it takes? I thought you didn't approve of killing.'

'Not as long as there's another way,' said Annie.

'What if there isn't?' said Lex.

'That's why you're part of the crew,' said Annie. 'You give us more options.'

Lex nodded slowly. 'I'll go along, for now.' He turned his gaze back to Murray. 'Sally dies, you die. You help, you live. Don't make me have to explain this again.'

'What could be fairer?' said Murray.

Lex stepped back and stared off into the distance, lost in his own thoughts. Annie and I moved cautiously together, to stand between Lex and Murray. The tension in the tent relaxed a little, but only a little.

'Before I can even point you in the right direction,' Murray said carefully, 'you're going to have to acquire one more person for your crew.'

'Who are we talking about?' I said. 'Some kind of specialist?'

'You could say that,' said Murray.

'Who did you have in mind?' said Annie.

'Polly Perkins,' said Murray.

'Oh, hell,' I said. 'Her? Really?'

Annie looked at me. 'You know this person?'

'Only by reputation,' I said. 'And not in a good way.'

'I sort of got that,' said Annie. 'What's wrong with her?'

'Polly is a first-class tracker,' I said. 'The word on the scene is that she can find anything or anyone. She also has a reputation for being loud, arrogant and a complete pain in the arse to work with.'

'I'd say that sums her up nicely,' said Murray. 'But you're going to need her particular skill set to rescue Sally.'

I glared at Murray. 'Convince me.'

'Coldheart is holding Sally prisoner with the rest of his treasures,' said Murray. 'In the heart of a great labyrinth, deep in the old city underneath Seattle. The Damned can handle the guards, and you and Annie can out-think all the traps and hidden defences, but you're going to need Polly to guide you through the twists and turns of the maze.'

'What's at the centre of this labyrinth?' said Annie. 'A fortress, a vault, a prison?'

'I can't see that far,' said Murray.

'Where do we find Polly?' I said.

Murray shrugged. 'She likes to keep on the move. I can tell you where she is right now, but you've got less than an hour before she'll be gone. My price for her current location is the same as before, Gideon; you have to promise you'll always protect me from the Damned. Whatever happens.'

I looked at him thoughtfully. 'You're not usually this nervous, Murray. Would I be right in thinking there are still some things about your involvement with this that haven't come to light yet? Things that, when they do eventually emerge, will make Lex even more mad at you than he is now?'

Murray sighed and seemed to slump in on himself. He looked suddenly older and a lot less mystic. Like a man too tired to play the games he used to be famous for. I admired the performance but wasn't sure I believed any of it. Murray was a con man, first and foremost, which meant that, like the magician he seemed to be, he would only ever allow you to see what he wanted you to.

'It's a hard world sometimes,' said Murray. 'We all do what we have to, to get by.'

'What have you done, Murray?' I said. 'Talk to me. You know the truth will out.'

'Not if I can help it,' said Murray.

'I could beat it out of you,' said Lex.

Murray sneered at him. 'I'm the only hope you have of ever seeing Sally again. Hark! Is that a clock I hear ticking?'

I wasn't sure I believed that, either. Murray could be bluffing. But there was no denying the man knew things. That was why we'd come to him. I looked reproachfully at Murray.

'I thought we were friends?'

'Of course we are, Gideon. But this is business. And a matter of basic survival. Give me your word that you'll stand between me and the Damned, and I will give you everything you need to rescue Sally. Try to short-change me, and I'll hang every single one of you out to dry. It's not like I'm asking for money – just a favour.'

'Your prevaricating could put Sally's life at risk,' I said. 'Do you really want to make enemies out of the legendarily dangerous people in this tent?'

Murray shrugged. 'I have so many deadly enemies I wouldn't even notice a few more.'

'And you trust me to keep you alive?'

Murray smiled. 'I have the utmost faith in you, Gideon.'

'You always did know how to fight dirty.' I sighed heavily. 'I seem to be making a lot of promises lately that I just know will come back to bite me on the arse at some future point. All right, you have my word. Tell me where we can find Polly, and I will protect you from the Damned for as long as necessary.'

Lex didn't look at me, but his quiet voice filled the tent. 'Thank you, Gideon.'

Because he couldn't bend to ask Murray for the help he needed, but I could. On his behalf.

'You'll find Polly Perkins at the Perfumed Alarm Clock,' said Murray. 'That's a nightclub in Paddington. She's their featured dancer.'

'What's the catch?' said Annie.

Murray raised an eyebrow. 'What makes you think there's a catch?'

'I've met you,' said Annie.

Murray nodded understandingly and flashed her a smile that held a lot of his old charm. If anything, that made me trust him even less. We were being set up for something; I could smell it. But it wasn't as if we had a choice.

'There is a catch,' said Murray. 'But it's not one of my making. Polly isn't going to want to go with you. Or do anything you want her to do. She hates working with other people and won't give a damn about saving Switch It Sally. Because Polly doesn't give a damn about anyone but herself. Good luck getting her to change her mind, because as far as I know, no one has ever been able to do that.'

Lex looked at Murray. 'I think I can persuade her to do the right thing.'

Murray showed him the kind of smile that all but shouts, *I know something you don't know*. But the smile faltered and fell apart in the face of the Damned's cold certainty.

'I really would love to see the two of you go head to head,' said Murray. 'Because it doesn't matter how bad you are, there's always someone worse. And Polly is in a class all of her own.'

I shook my head. 'Of all the people you could have wished on us, you had to go with Polly Perkins . . . I will make you pay for this, Murray.'

'People have been saying that for years,' Murray said cheerfully. 'And I'm still here. When you've talked the famously recalcitrant Polly into joining your merry little crew, and I would dearly love to be a fly on the wall for that conversation, then I will contact you and arrange our next meeting. Where I will present you with a way into Coldheart's labyrinth of such an unexpected nature that I can positively guarantee no one will see you coming. Then all you have to do is find a way past the minotaur.'

'Hold everything,' I said. 'Go back and go previous. What minotaur? You didn't say anything about a minotaur!'

Murray grinned. 'Come on, Gideon, you know there's always a monster at the heart of a labyrinth. It's traditional.'

Before I could press him on that, Murray smiled happily round the tent and drew himself up to his full height.

'Hello, I must be going.'

And without a single magical word or mystical gesture, Murray the Mentalist was gone. Taking the tent with him.

Annie, the Damned and I were left standing on a deserted Brighton Pier. It was night, under a full moon, the dark sky full of stars. Annie and I shuddered at the sudden chill. The Damned didn't. I looked quickly up and down the pier, but there was no one else around. The day was over, the pier was locked up, and the shopkeepers and the crowds had departed. The sound of the sea was very loud in the quiet.

'Nice exit,' said Annie.

'I thought so,' I said.

'He's keeping things from us, isn't he?' said Annie.

'Of course he is,' I said. 'That's what he does. If only so that he can sell us more information at a later date.'

'Such as?' said Annie.

'To start with, why did he point the finger at Sally in the first place? She's not the only one with her particular gift. Remember Tommy Two Way? Someone like him could have had that rock out of our shop, and we would never have known it was gone until we went looking for it. No, there has to be more to this than we're seeing.'

Annie lowered her voice. 'Are you really ready to protect Murray from the Damned, whatever it takes?'

'I gave Murray my word,' I said. 'Though it would help if I knew why he was so sure he'd need protecting.'

'I would have thought that was obvious,' said Annie.

I smiled. 'You don't know Murray. If he's that worried, he must have done a lot more than he's admitted so far.'

'We have to get Sally back,' said Lex.

'And stay alive while we do it,' I said.

'Perfectionist,' said Lex.

'Sidney!' Annie said loudly. 'Will you please come and get us! It's freezing here!'

The standing mirror appeared before us, dropping into reality like a bad coin into a slot machine.

'What am I, your nanny? I should start charging you by the mile.'

'I thought you needed your beauty rest?' I said.

'I couldn't sleep,' said the mirror.

'We need to go to Paddington, Sidney,' said Annie. 'A nightclub called the Perfumed Alarm Clock.'

'I know that club,' said the mirror, just a bit surprisingly. 'It's a real dive, with all the charm of a punch in the face. You don't want to go there. I know some much better joints, with atmosphere and everything . . .'

'We have to go to the Perfumed Alarm Clock,' I said firmly. 'This is work, not pleasure. And needs must when the devil vomits on your blue suede shoes.'

The mirror hesitated. 'Could I go in with you?'

'It sounds a bit rough, Sidney,' said Annie. 'You might get broken.'

'We'll tell you all about it when we get back,' I said.

The mirror sighed heavily. 'I never get to go to the fun places.'

FIVE
Not Fighting, Only Playing

One by one, we passed through the mirror and found ourselves on a London street full of sound and fury, and people determined to have a good time no matter what. Nightclubs lined both sides of the street as far as our eyes could see, in every conceivable fashion and flavour. Their blazing neon signs were almost unbearably garish, and the club exteriors had been decorated in every shade under the sun or the moon, like the alluringly attractive petals of a poisonous plant.

One glance around was enough to assure me this wasn't the kind of area where you came for a nice night out. These were the kind of clubs that catered exclusively for those with darker tastes; where the good times would always be flavoured with chemical enhancements, and usually ended in screaming matches and fistfights up and down the pavements in the early hours of the morning. Clubs for those with hot blood and hotter passions, no restraint and less conscience.

Annie tapped me on the arm. 'This doesn't look like Paddington.'

'Not any part of it I know,' I said. 'Maybe it only comes out at night.'

'Are we at least in the right place?'

I pointed across the road, to where the doors to the Perfumed Alarm Clock stood wide open, because the entrances to even the most private hells always are. The club's neon sign blazed like candy with a razor blade hidden inside, and the steel and glass frontage looked as if it had been built to keep people in, as well as out. A lengthy queue of the fashionably attired waited impatiently to be admitted, sharing the latest gossip and plotting on how best to start a little of their own. Some of the would-be revellers were chasing down handfuls of pills with passed-around bottles, while others studied passing would-be revellers with thoughtful, hungry looks.

'Not exactly upmarket, is it?' said Annie.

'But very definitely the kind of place Murray would know,' I said. 'It's probably as big a con as he is: offering all kinds of attractions with no intention of delivering on any of them.'

I looked around for the standing mirror, but there was no sign of him.

'Sidney! Get your reflective arse back here, right now!'

The mirror slunk into existence beside me. 'What do you want? I was in the bath!'

I didn't rise to the bait, just pointed across the road at the Perfumed Alarm Clock.

'We needed to appear inside the club, not standing around on the street.'

'Then you should have said so, shouldn't you?' said Sidney. And he disappeared again.

I considered calling him back so I could breathe on his surface and write rude words in the mist, but I rose above it. Self-control is a major part of every heist. And there was always the chance he might enjoy it. I turned to Annie and shrugged. She smiled.

'He's only sulking because we wouldn't take him in with us.'

'They wouldn't have allowed him in anyway,' I said. 'He wasn't properly dressed.'

'And we are?' said Lex, looking down at his suit. 'It's been a long time since I was fashionable, but I'm fairly certain this isn't it.'

'They'll let us in,' I said confidently.

'How can you be so sure?' said Annie.

I had to smile. 'Because there isn't a bouncer in London who could keep us out.'

I took another look around, testing the waters before I committed myself. The whole street scene was wild and wondrous, packed with night people at their play, as casually cruel as kittens, but without the charm. The latest sounds blasted out of every door, fighting it out in a Darwinian struggle for enticement, offering hot and cold running decadence and sin on tap. Bright young things smiled knowingly as they paraded up and down the street in their finest clothes, feral peacocks on display and queens of the night with cold, cold smiles.

The long queues outside the clubs were held at bay by large muscular gentlemen in formal suits, there to make sure that only the right sort of people got in. The rich and the fashionable, the famous and the connected, because there was no point in fleecing people unless they were worth the effort. Some tried to argue, shouting, 'Don't you know who I am?' I always thought the answer to that was implicit in the question. Hard, unyielding faces at the doors made it clear that they had heard it all before and hadn't been impressed the first time. Bouncers, so called because they liked to make bets on how far someone would bounce after they were thrown out.

'Do you have a plan to get us in past the Neanderthals on steroids?' said Annie.

'We don't need a plan,' I said. 'We have Lex.'

Annie smiled. 'I suppose we could always use him as a battering ram.'

I suddenly realized that the standing mirror had returned, lurking apologetically beside me. The people streaming past apparently couldn't see him, because they didn't even glance in his direction, although, interestingly, no one tried to walk through him. I gave Sidney a hard look, and he started talking before I could get a word out.

'Just thought I'd make it clear, in case you were wondering, that I couldn't get you inside the Perfumed Alarm Clock because it has security protections in place that could stomp all over me with hob-nailed boots. So if you want to call for a lift home, you'll have to come back out into the street to do it. You'd be better off calling for a taxi. Always assuming you could persuade one to come and pick you up in an area like this. And you should definitely bear in mind that any Uber driver who would agree to come here is probably someone you shouldn't get into a car with anyway.'

'Sidney . . .' I said.

'All this shuttling you around is not good for my karma!'

the mirror said loudly. 'I am an oracle and a source of wisdom, not a travel agency.'

'All right, oh wondrous oracle,' I said. 'Tell us something useful.'

Sidney orientated himself so his surface was facing the Perfumed Alarm Clock and then stood there silently. Either because he was thinking or because he wasn't sure what he could usefully contribute.

'When you get in there,' he said finally, 'don't talk to any strangers, don't eat the faerie food and, above all, watch your backs.'

I gave him a hard look. 'You said you knew this club.'

'Only by reputation,' said Sidney. 'It's been a long time since I was in a position to go dancing.'

'Have you heard anything about this Perkins person that we're supposed to be looking for?' said Annie.

'Polly Perkins?' said Sidney. 'Oh, yes . . . Watch out for her. She's a real animal.'

He laughed loudly and blinked out of existence again. His final snigger lingered on the air, like the smile on the face of the Cheshire Cat.

'In his own weird and warped way, I think Sidney was trying to tell us something,' said Annie.

'Why are we standing around here?' Lex said heavily. 'If we need this Polly, let's go and get her.'

I drew Lex's attention to the oversized bouncers guarding the doors, and he gave them the kind of look a professional always bestows on the merely talented amateur.

'Stick close,' said Lex. 'But don't get in the way.'

He headed straight for the club entrance, and everyone in the street immediately fell back to give him plenty of room. Because they could tell Lex was quite happy to walk through anyone who got in his way. They didn't have to know he was the Damned to know he was dangerous. Annie and I fell in behind Lex, ready to use him as a human shield if necessary. I pride myself on being able to talk my way past most obstacles, but these bouncers looked as though they'd been trained not to listen to reasonable arguments.

We strode past the waiting queue, and even though it must

have been obvious we were going to cut in, none of them challenged our right to do so. Most were too busy muttering to each other about Lex. A few made comments about his suit but were quickly hushed by their friends, who knew violence about to happen when they saw it.

Lex walked right up to the bouncers at the door, and I got ready to sweep Annie out of the way if one or more bodies came flying in our direction. Instead, the bouncers just put on their most professional smiles, pushed the doors open and stepped courteously to one side so Lex could enter.

'An honour to have you here, sir,' said the larger of the bouncers. 'The noted and illustrious Damned is always a welcome guest in this establishment! Drinks are on the house! Please try not to break anyone important.'

The second bouncer started to say something, but the other glared him into silence.

'Don't you dare ask the Damned for an autograph.'

Lex ignored both of them and strode on into the club. Annie and I went to follow him inside, but the bouncers moved quickly to stand together, filling the doorway with a wall of muscle. They stared us down with closed-off faces, defying us to get past them. I thought about my time pen and all the indignities I could inflict on them while Time was stopped, but this didn't seem like a good moment to be attracting attention.

'You know who that was,' I said, nodding to the disappearing Damned. 'We're with him.'

'We're his minders,' said Annie.

'Right,' I said. 'We keep him from making trouble. Or wrecking entire establishments.'

The bouncers stirred uneasily and glanced at each other. The larger of the two drew himself up to say something intimidating, only to break off abruptly as Lex appeared behind him and breathed in his ear.

'They're with me.'

The bouncers stepped resignedly to one side, and Annie and I strode past them like visiting dignitaries. I couldn't help noticing that nothing was said to us about drinks being on the house. I paused at the doors and considered the bouncers thoughtfully.

'Why is this place called the Perfumed Alarm Clock? The name doesn't make any sense.'

'And Spearmint Rhino does?' said the larger bouncer. 'The new management inherited the name when he bought the club.'

'Sixties revival,' said the other bouncer. 'That Austin Powers has a lot to answer for.'

'It's all seventies disco now,' said the first.

'Nostalgia isn't what it used to be.'

The larger bouncer looked at me hopefully. 'I don't suppose you could give us a hint as to why the Damned has chosen to grace us with his presence?'

'Only we would like some idea of which way to duck,' said the other.

'He's here to see Polly Perkins,' I said.

'Oh, shit,' said the larger bouncer.

'I think we should go home early,' said the other.

'You stand your ground, Ron. Our dad went to a lot of trouble to get us these jobs, after what happened at the old place.'

'But it's all going to kick off!'

'That's what we're here for! And don't you dare start snivelling, or I will slap the life out of you.'

Annie and I left them discussing the situation and moved on into the club.

'This isn't going to go well, is it?' said Annie.

'Does it ever, where Lex is concerned?'

'Not that I've noticed,' said Annie.

The club interior was all flashing lights and pounding music. Men in white suits and women in clingy dresses threw themselves around the dance floor to the Bee Gees' greatest hits, showing off moves they'd learned from watching movies so old they were practically period pieces. They danced with more enthusiasm than style but seemed to be enjoying themselves.

There were a few Ziggy Stardusts and Aladdin Sanes, which at least showed a little ambition.

Annie moved in close, so she could bellow into my ear over the music.

'This is my idea of Hell. Dancing is supposed to be fun, not a physical workout.'

'At least the crowd will make for good cover,' I yelled back.

'How are we supposed to find Polly in all of this?' said Annie. 'Murray didn't even give us a description.'

'He seemed to think we'd know her when we saw her,' I said.

The Damned was walking straight across the dance floor; without quite looking directly at him, all the dancers arranged to give him plenty of space. He passed through the crowd like a predator at a watering hole who didn't happen to be hungry, just at the moment. It was clear that many of the dancers knew who he was, and I could see admiration in their faces along with the fear. If Lex noticed, he didn't give a damn.

'Maybe we should go back and ask the bouncers where to look for Polly?' said Annie.

'Given how they reacted to her name, I don't think they'd want to do anything that might upset her,' I said.

And then I broke off as I spotted a young Indian woman dancing alone on a raised stage in a golden spotlight. She was drop-dead gorgeous, and she knew it. Well over six feet tall, lean and muscular, with long black hair that swept this way and that as she whipped her head back and forth, she danced entirely naked, bare feet slamming against the stage to the rhythm of the music. Drops of sweat flew from her dark skin with every impact. Her mouth was stretched in a fierce grin, but her eyes were far away, lost in the dance and the moment. She was surrounded by worshipful admirers doing their best to copy her moves, but none of them had the strength or the style to keep up with her.

'Is that Polly?' said Annie.

'I don't see any other featured dancer,' I said. 'And she does fit what I know of Polly's reputation.'

'A show-off?' Annie said sweetly.

'Mad, bad and dangerous to be near.'

'Just how well do you know her?' said Annie.

'I know she tracks down missing people,' I said. 'And locates rare objects. For a considerable fee.'

'Which we don't have,' said Annie. 'How are we going to persuade her to join us?'

'I'll think of something,' I said. 'It's what I do.'

'What if Lex gets to her first?'

'Then we look for something substantial to hide behind.'

Annie winced as the DJ cranked the volume up another notch.

'How can we talk to her with all this going on?'

I looked around. 'There must be a plug I can pull.'

I waved an arm to catch Lex's attention. He came plunging back through the dancers, and they parted like the Red Sea to let him pass. When he finally joined us, I pointed out the nude dancer, and the Damned gave me a *How the hell did I miss that?* look. I gestured for him to lean in close and yelled in his ear.

'We need to talk to Polly. Could you please do something about the music?'

Lex nodded and headed for the music decks. The DJ was dressed like Huggy Bear from the old *Starsky and Hutch* TV series, not a good look for an overweight white guy. Lex jumped up on to the raised stage, picked up the DJ's decks and threw them out on to the dance floor. The dancers scattered like startled birds as the decks exploded. Bits and pieces shot through the air like shrapnel, and the music stopped as if someone had just cut the Bee Gees' throats.

A terrible hush fell across the dance floor, as everyone stumbled to a halt. The DJ threw himself at Lex, so outraged by the destruction of his decks that he'd stopped paying attention to his self-preservation instincts. Lex grabbed the DJ out of mid-air with one hand and threw him at the dance floor. The DJ hit the crowd like a cannonball, sending people flying like skittles. None of those still on their feet paid them any attention; they only had eyes for Lex. He smiled down at them.

'Leave. While you still can.'

The crowd turned as one and raced for the exit. They might have thought they wanted to see the Damned in action, but once he'd turned his cold gaze on them, that was a whole different thing. The only reason they weren't fighting each

other to get to the doors first was that it might have slowed
them down.

The two bouncers appeared, shouldering their way through
the tide of frightened bodies and out on to the emptying dance
floor. Lex stared at them thoughtfully from the stage, and
the bouncers slammed to a halt. They knew when they were
outclassed. The last of the panicked crowd elbowed their way
through the doors, leaving the bouncers alone and exposed on
the dance floor. Lex jumped down from the stage, and they
huddled together for mutual support. Perhaps fortunately, a
middle-aged man in a baggy suit appeared through a side door,
took in what had happened to his paying crowd and glared at
the bouncers. They gestured helplessly at Lex. The management strode over to them and stabbed a finger at Lex.

'Do something!'

The larger bouncer shook his head. 'You're not paying us
enough to mess with the Damned. In fact, there isn't that
much money in the entire world. You want something done,
you do it.'

The management looked at the Damned and headed for the
exit. The bouncers were right behind him. And just like that,
the club was quiet and deserted. Lex came over to join us,
and we turned to face the only other person who hadn't left.

Polly Perkins stood alone on her stage, staring back at us
with dark and dangerous eyes. She made no move to step
down, but just threw her head back and planted her fists defiantly on her hips. She wasn't breathing hard, despite her recent
exertions, but she was glistening all over with sweat. She didn't
seem in the least embarrassed by her nudity; all I could see
in her face was a cold annoyance at having her dancing
interrupted.

We moved over to stand before her. I tried hard to appear
suave and civilized about the whole nakedness thing, while
Annie rose above it. Lex didn't give a damn. Polly scowled
fiercely down at us and seemed a little taken aback when it
didn't bother us in the least. She regarded us haughtily, like
a pagan goddess whose ritual had been interrupted by
barbarians, and when she finally addressed us, her voice was
low and husky with over- and undertones of menace.

'I was dancing!'

'You need to come with us,' said Lex.

Polly shook her head, and her long black hair danced for a moment. 'Not going to happen. Didn't anyone warn you about me?'

'I'm Gideon Sable,' I said. 'This is Annie Anybody, and this . . . is Lex Talon.'

Our names meant nothing to her, but Polly concentrated on Lex and finally nodded slowly.

'You're the Damned. What do you want?'

'He's with me,' I said quickly. 'I'm putting a crew together.'

'I don't do crews,' Polly said immediately. 'I work alone.'

'But I can offer you excitement and adventure,' I said. 'A chance to bring down a really bad man and rescue a damsel in distress. I will take you places you have never been, show you wonders you have never seen – and make sure you get a good chance to steal most of them.'

Polly looked at Annie. 'Talks nice, doesn't he?' She turned her dark gaze back to me, cool and collected and entirely unconcerned. 'Not interested. I turn down all kinds of people, no matter what they offer. I don't work for the money or the glory; it's just something to keep me occupied when I'm not dancing.'

'You can dance any day,' said Lex.

He grabbed her bare arm in his huge hand, ready to haul her down off the stage if she resisted. Polly jerked her arm free with surprising strength and growled at Lex, a deep, disturbing animal sound. Lex started to climb up on to the stage. Polly planted a foot on his chest and thrust him away with such force that he fell sprawling on his back. Polly laughed loudly as Lex scrambled on to his feet again.

'Getting old, Mr Damned?'

'Someone bring me a sack,' said Lex. 'She's leaving.'

And then he stopped, as black fur swept over Polly's skin. Her back arched, her muscles bulged, and bones cracked loudly as her arms and legs lengthened. Her face stretched forward into a muzzle, long pointed ears thrust up, and grey lips pulled back to reveal sharp pointed teeth. Vicious claws protruded from her hands, and her eyes glowed golden.

In just a few moments, the dancer was gone, replaced by a werewolf in thick black fur.

I looked at Annie. 'I will get Sidney for this. *She's a real animal . . .*'

Polly tilted back her lupine head and howled mockingly. The smell of hot animal musk was heavy on the air. She lowered her head to glare at us with her golden eyes and growled again, deep in her throat. I could feel the sound reverberating in my bones. Lex looked at me.

'No wonder she always works on her own. She's a lone wolf.'

I stared at him. 'All these years to develop a sense of humour, and it's a twisted one.'

He shrugged. 'At least now we know what makes her such a great tracker. I'll keep her occupied; you find me a collar and leash.'

The werewolf threw herself at Lex, her clawed hands reaching for his throat. He grabbed a black-furred arm, swung the werewolf over his head and slammed her against the floor. The impact would have driven all the breath from anyone else's lungs, but the werewolf just brought a leg sweeping across with vicious speed, cutting Lex's feet out from under him. He hit the floor hard, and the werewolf leaped on top of him, bared teeth straining for his throat. Lex slammed a forearm against the werewolf's throat, forcing the teeth back and away from him.

The two of them fought each other with terrible intensity. The werewolf kept pressing the attack, but even her strength and speed were no match for the Damned. He might not be wearing his armour, but the man who had killed so many people who needed killing was still a force to be reckoned with. The werewolf and the Damned rolled back and forth across the dance floor, first one on top and then the other.

Annie and I watched it all from a safe distance. I studied the fight carefully until Annie stirred uneasily at my side.

'Shouldn't we be doing something?'

'They seem to be doing fine on their own,' I said.

'I mean, shouldn't we try to stop them before they kill each other?' said Annie.

'I don't think that's going to happen,' I said. 'They're not fighting, only playing.'

Annie turned to look at me. 'What?'

'If Lex thought he was in serious danger, he would have put on his armour,' I said. 'And if Polly really wanted him dead, her teeth and claws would have found a weak spot by now. I think they're just fascinated at finding someone who can keep up with them.'

Even as I said that, Lex and Polly broke apart, rolled away from each other and rose quickly to their feet. Neither of them was breathing hard, and their eyes met steadily. The cold gaze of the Damned and the golden eyes of the werewolf. Polly straightened up out of her werewolf's crouch, and fur, teeth and claws disappeared. She stretched slowly as her nude figure reappeared.

'So, Lex,' she said, 'you really are everything they say you are. What does the Damned want with me?'

'My wife has been kidnapped,' said Lex. 'I need your help to get her back. After I've killed the man responsible, you're welcome to help yourself to anything you want from his treasure house.'

'I don't need bribing,' Polly said easily. 'I just fancy fighting alongside the Damned.'

'Then join the crew,' said Lex.

Polly looked across at me. 'Will this be dangerous?'

'Wouldn't surprise me,' I said.

'Then I'm in,' said Polly Perkins.

We had to wait while Polly retrieved her clothes from behind the stage. She quickly pulled them on, as unselfconscious about getting dressed in front of strangers as she had been about dancing naked in front of a crowd. After a quick glance at Annie, I decided to look in a different direction. Lex moved in beside me and lowered his voice.

'If Sally even suspected I was interested in another woman, she would switch out my heart and leave a large stone in its place.'

'I can believe that,' I said.

Polly ended up in black motorcycle leathers with a great

many jangling zips, knee-length boots, and a black silk scarf around her neck. She slouched over to us and fixed Lex with her dark gaze.

'Where are we going?'

Lex gestured to me. 'Ask him – he gives the orders.'

Polly looked me up and down. 'Why?'

'Because he is Gideon Sable, master thief,' Annie said sternly.

Polly just shrugged. 'Why does that put him in charge?'

'Because I'm the man with the plan,' I said. 'And we're going to need a really good one to bring down the collector called Coldheart.'

'I don't usually bother with plans,' said Polly. 'Mostly, I just follow my instincts and my nose, and rip the guts out of whatever gets in my way.'

'It amazes me you've survived this long,' I said.

'Gideon knows what he's doing,' said Lex. 'I follow him.'

Polly shrugged again. It seemed to be her default response to most things.

'I don't give a damn for the old team spirit. But if the Damned is involved, I'm expecting mayhem and body counts on an unprecedented scale. All the things that make a girl's heart beat that little bit faster. So, team leader, where are we going?'

'America,' I said. 'The city of Seattle, to be exact.'

'Cool!' said Polly. 'Why do you need me?'

'Best not to discuss that in public,' I said.

Polly looked around the empty dance floor. 'What public?'

'You can never tell who might be listening,' said Annie.

'Come with us, Polly,' I said, 'and we'll go and meet the man who told us we'd need you.'

'Which me?' said Polly. 'The tracker or the wolf?'

'That's one of the things I plan on asking him,' I said.

'I thought you were in charge?' said Polly.

'I am,' I said. 'But he knows things. Shall we go?'

Polly shrugged. 'Why not?'

We walked out of the club to find the street crammed with excited onlookers. Not just the dancers who'd fled from the

Perfumed Alarm Clock but, from the look of it, patrons from every club up and down the street. Word had got around. Packed shoulder to shoulder, the crowd cheered and screamed enthusiastically when they saw Polly walking in company with the Damned. One of their own had just made it to the big time. A sea of arms rose up as they pointed phones in our direction. Annie and I eased casually in behind Lex.

Polly strutted and posed and punched the air triumphantly. Lex just stared back at the crowd, completely indifferent, and that very detachment made him even cooler in their eyes. I wondered how they would have felt if they could have seen him after the Murder Bureau massacre, soaked in the blood of his victims. I got the feeling they would have liked that even more.

I called out to Sidney, and the mirror appeared in front of me.

'I see you found Polly,' Sidney said innocently. 'Is she everything you thought she'd be?'

I glared at him accusingly. 'You knew all along that she was a werewolf!'

'Of course,' said Sidney. 'Doesn't everyone?'

'I should paint you over and lock you in the attic.'

'Do we have an attic?' said Annie.

'I'll build one.'

'But then how would you get around?' Sidney said craftily. 'I take it you do need me to transfer you somewhere?'

Before I could say anything, the surface of the mirror changed suddenly, to show Murray smiling back at me.

'Now the team is complete, step on through, and I will set you on the road to where you need to be.'

'Hey!' Sidney said indignantly. 'How did you hijack my coordinates! Get out of me!'

'Just go with the flow, Sidney,' I said. 'Murray's running this show, for the moment.'

I led the way into the mirror, and the crowd cheered again. The sound cut off sharply as we suddenly found ourselves somewhere else.

*   *   *

The bare featureless room seemed very drab and grey after the technicolour excesses of Paddington's club scene.

Lex scowled around him. He didn't like surprises. Polly was fascinated by the sudden change in location and padded swiftly around the room, sniffing at the air. Annie immediately looked for an exit, because life had taught her to be practical and paranoid. There was no obvious door, no windows, and the only illumination came from a single bare light bulb. We could have been miles underground or at the top of a building. The perfect prison cell. The only furniture consisted of five plastic chairs arranged in a circle, and the mirror standing silently behind us.

'Where's Murray?' Annie said suspiciously.

'He'll be here,' I said. 'He never could resist a chance to show off.'

'We need to find Sally,' said Lex.

'That's what this meeting is all about,' I said.

'Who's Sally?' said Polly.

'My wife,' said Lex.

Polly stared at him incredulously. 'You mean the rumours are true? You actually married Switch It Sally?'

'You know her?' I said.

'Oh, everyone knows her,' said Polly. 'That light-fingered little cow still owes me money.'

'Then you'd better help us get her back,' I said. 'If you ever want to see your money again.'

'If she's involved, my fee just doubled,' said Polly.

'There is no fee,' Annie said sweetly.

'Then why should I help?' said Polly.

'For the chance to fight at my side,' said Lex.

'And a chance to loot one of the biggest treasure houses in the world,' I said.

Polly flashed me a grin. 'If I'd known crews could be this much fun, I'd have joined one ages ago.'

'But if you betray us,' said Lex, 'I will have you stuffed and mounted and put on display where you used to dance.'

'Well,' said Polly, 'that goes without saying.'

Annie moved in beside me and lowered her voice. 'Could we get out of here . . . if we had to?'

'We still have Sidney,' I said, just as quietly. 'Are you feeling trapped?'

'Just a bit.'

I turned to the mirror. 'Sidney, do you have any idea where you've brought us?'

The standing mirror cleared its throat apologetically. 'Sorry, sir, but I am not Sidney. I am Albert.'

We all turned to stare at the mirror. Now that I looked closely, I could see this mirror was framed in a darker wood, and its whole appearance was somewhat shabbier, as though the world had treated it roughly.

'What happened to Sidney?' said Annie.

'Mr Murray intercepted him, miss,' said Albert. 'And substituted me. I work for Mr Murray. Indentured servant, you might say.'

I looked at him sternly. 'Why have you brought us here, Albert?'

'Because this is where Mr Murray wants you to be, sir. Please take a seat and make yourselves comfortable. I'm sure Mr Murray will be along shortly.'

'How many talking mirrors are there?' said Annie.

'I'm sure I couldn't say, miss,' said Albert. 'How many people have been bad?'

Annie looked ready to press him on that, but I cut in.

'He's just trying to distract you. He isn't going to tell us anything Murray doesn't want us to know. Isn't that right, Albert?'

'I can see you've spent time with Mr Murray before, sir,' said the mirror. 'Please take a seat. I would offer you refreshments, but there aren't any.'

I decided I'd better set an example, to calm everyone's nerves. I didn't want anyone getting edgy. That would give Murray the advantage. I moved over to the circle of chairs and sat down, and one by one the others came and joined me. Lex's chair creaked loudly under his weight. Polly curled up on her chair, utterly indifferent to her surroundings. I arranged mine so I could keep an eye on the mirror. Annie leaned in beside me.

'Why are you being so cautious, Gideon?'

'I think I've had enough surprises for one day,' I said.

'Don't you trust Murray?'

'Up to a point.'

'But he's your friend.'

'Depends on who he's being,' I said. 'You're always you, under your various personas. Murray can be very different people. I always know where I am with Madam Osiris; Murray, not so much.'

'That's just weird,' said Annie.

'You should know.'

Annie looked around the empty room. 'Why do you think he brought us here?'

'Perhaps he feels the need for a secure setting before he unburdens himself of Coldheart's secrets.'

'What's the deal with this Murray?' said Polly, just to make it clear she wasn't going to be left out of the conversation.

I brought her up to speed on Sally, the stone and the sirens' song, taking care to emphasize just how dangerous Coldheart and his people could be.

'As long as I get to strut my stuff alongside the Damned, I'm cool,' Polly said airily. She turned abruptly to Lex. 'Although I have to ask, why did you marry Switch It Sally of all people?'

'She isn't scared of me,' said Lex.

'Neither am I,' said Polly.

'You don't know me,' said Lex.

Polly shrugged and rocked back and forth on her chair. 'Who exactly is this Murray, anyway?'

'Murray the Mentalist,' I said.

'Never heard of him,' said Polly.

'He's heard of you,' I said. 'But then Murray's heard of everyone. Knowledge is his currency.'

'Did I just hear you say you don't trust him?' said Polly.

'I trust his information,' I said, 'because he wouldn't lower himself to lie to us. Of course, what he tells us might not be complete or as helpful as it seems.'

Polly thought about that for a moment. 'Is there someone else who could help us?'

'Murray knows what we need to know,' I said. 'Which puts him in the driving seat, for the moment.'

'You've got silver on you,' Polly said abruptly. 'I can smell it.'

'I believe in being prepared,' I said.

'You think you could take me?' said Polly.

'The Damned follows my orders,' I said. 'What does that tell you?'

Polly looked at Lex, who nodded solemnly. Polly turned back to me and grinned broadly.

'This crew gets more interesting by the moment.'

I smiled back at her. 'Wild thing, I think I love you.'

'Down, boy,' said Annie.

Murray stepped out of the standing mirror and quickly checked out the room. He was still wearing his dinner suit and black silk turban, but now the blood-red jewel blazed fiercely. Presumably, he'd remembered to change the batteries. Murray smiled around the circle of chairs, in his element at last: the man who knew things, with an audience ready to be impressed. There was a definite bounce to his step as he came over to join us, looking very pleased with himself.

'You actually persuaded Polly to join your crew, Gideon! How on earth did you manage that?'

'I offered her something she wanted,' I said.

Murray looked at me expectantly, but I just smiled calmly back at him.

'I'm impressed,' Murray said finally. 'Polly Perkins isn't known for playing nicely with others.'

Polly looked down her nose at him. 'Who's the old creep?'

Murray fixed her with his best cold stare. 'I could make all your hair fall out with a single word. So mind your manners, little wolf girl, unless you want to be the most naked werewolf ever.'

Polly stirred uneasily on her chair. Something about Murray disturbed her instincts, and that intrigued me. I'd never thought of Murray as dangerous before, only devious. But it had been a long time since I'd last seen the man, and people do change.

Murray rubbed his hands together briskly. 'Let's get this briefing done. I'm really not comfortable being out in the open, so the sooner I can rush off and be somebody else the better.'

'Weird,' said Polly.

'You have no idea,' said Murray.

He sat down on the last remaining chair, crossed his legs elegantly and shot both his cuffs. I braced myself. Murray loved to lecture people, especially when they had no choice but to listen. And he did so love to spring his little surprises.

'Coldheart specializes in collectibles of a musical nature,' he said. 'He has spent most of his life hunting down rare musical recordings, instruments and associated items. His collection of such things is said to be the biggest in the world, but his appetite remains insatiable.'

'What is Coldheart's real name?' I said.

Murray shot me a look, to make it clear he wasn't happy at being interrupted.

'I don't think anyone knows. Coldheart never appears in public. He always uses other people to acquire the precious things he wants, and he surrounds himself with all the protections necessary to make sure he can hang on to them. He has no conscience, no restraint, and he never stops going after something until it's his.

'There are no photos of the man, and what descriptions there are vary widely. The man is a mystery, and he likes it that way. People who try to dig into his past tend to disappear. His security chiefs, Cleopatra Bones and her husband Malice, give Coldheart a very long reach.'

'Other people must have gone after his treasure house before this,' I said. 'I know some who would take its very existence as a challenge.'

'Certain other collectors, who saw themselves as robbed or cheated, have sent agents to take their revenge on Coldheart,' said Murray. 'Not one of them has ever been seen again.'

Polly sat up straight for the first time. 'You make him sound seriously dangerous.'

'He is,' said Murray.

'Excellent!' said Polly. And then she looked at me thoughtfully. 'Do you honestly believe Coldheart can get a song out of a stone?'

'The important thing is that he believes it,' I said.

'Coldheart has invested a lot of money in state-of-the-art audio technology,' said Murray. 'Designed to recover all manner of sounds from physical objects.'

'Like a stone tape?' said Polly.

'If you like,' said Murray.

'Why is he so obsessed about the sirens' song?' said Annie.

'He wants to hear it,' said Murray.

'You do seem to know an awful lot about this, Murray,' I said. 'By any chance, have you been planning your own assault on Coldheart's treasure house?'

'I might have done a little quiet research,' said Murray. 'I don't want anything that man has, but for my own reasons . . . it would please me to see Coldheart brought down.'

'So you're using us,' I said.

'Just as you're using me,' said Murray. 'Isn't that what old friends are for? Now, if I may continue . . .'

'By all means,' I said. 'Don't let me stop you.'

'Coldheart is based in Seattle,' said Murray. 'Or, to be more exact, in a complex labyrinth set deep under the streets of the modern city. His treasure house lies right at the heart of this maze, protected by all kinds of guards, traps and deadly defences. And no, I can't tell you what any of them are. No one knows. That's the point. The only thing I can be sure of is the minotaur.'

'An actual minotaur?' I said.

Murray shrugged. 'There are only so many ways I can say it: *No one knows for sure.* The only thing the gossips and whisperers agree on is that there is definitely something monstrous lying in wait at the heart of the maze. "Minotaur" is the name most people have put to it. And given Coldheart's obsession with the past, who's to say he hasn't acquired the modern equivalent? There's never any shortage of monsters, in our line of business.'

'This is so cool!' said Polly, bouncing up and down on her seat. 'When my friends hear I've taken down a minotaur, they will eat their own heads with jealousy!'

'All I have is the name,' said Murray. 'It doesn't necessarily mean a large gentleman with a bull's head.'

'We know how to deal with monsters,' I said.

'We just took down a gorgon and a chronovore,' said Annie, her voice studiedly casual.

'Really?' said Polly. 'Cool beans!'

'And it does help that we have our very own monster in the crew,' I said.

Polly bristled. 'I am not a monster!'

'I was thinking of Lex,' I said.

The Damned just nodded.

'Whatever the creature on guard turns out to be,' said Murray, 'see if you can bring some part of it back as a souvenir. I know collectors who would pay good money for such an item.'

'So do I,' I said. 'Which is why I'll be hanging on to every-thing I bring back. Is there anything else you can tell us, Murray?'

'The only people who have personal contact with the man are Cleopatra Bones and Malice,' said Murray. 'They run his security and act as personal bodyguards. Very scary individuals. Between them, they're supposed to have killed more people than the Damned. And they don't have his armour.'

Lex looked coldly at Murray. 'You're sure Sally is being held at the centre of the maze?'

'Along with Coldheart's collection, yes,' said Murray.

'Then we go in and get her,' said Lex. 'And walk right through anything and anyone that gets in our way.'

'Isn't he amazing?' Polly said happily.

'He really is,' I said. 'But I don't like not knowing what defences and protections we might be facing. There are some things even you couldn't stand against, Lex, and it sounds like Coldheart could afford to buy them.'

'That's where I come in,' said Polly.

'And what if the guards have silver bullets?' I said. 'What if there are special traps and defences, designed to deal with people like us?'

'All I can tell you is what I've heard,' said Murray.

I thought about it. I don't normally believe in starting a heist without a detailed plan, but I didn't possess enough information, and there wasn't time to do the research. If things really were as they seemed, Sally's life could be in danger. And I couldn't hold Lex back much longer. I gave Murray a hard look.

'Do you at least have a map of the labyrinth?'

'I can't even provide you with a ball of thread,' said Murray.

'There has to be something more you can tell us,' said Annie.

'Coldheart lives inside his treasure house,' said Murray. 'He can't bear to be apart from his collection. He never leaves the place. If you can make your way through the maze, break into the fortress and rescue Sally, you will be the first outsiders to set your eyes on the supernatural community's very own Howard Hughes. And, Gideon, if you're going, you have to go now.'

Lex stood up, and everyone's eyes went to him.

'We're going.'

'You have to understand,' Murray said carefully, 'that it could already be too late for Sally.'

'If anything has happened to my wife, I will kill Coldheart,' said Lex. 'And all of his people.'

The cold certainty in his voice struck us all silent.

'If anyone could do that, it would be you,' Murray said finally.

'Let's look on the bright side,' I said. 'We could come back with Sally, and the rock, and enough treasure to make all of us incredibly rich.'

'Hold it,' said Annie. 'Before we go anywhere . . . I want to know why you're being so helpful, Murray. And don't give me any of that *old friends* bullshit.'

'Because I was the one who put Sally in danger,' said Murray. 'I threw her to the wolves, to save my own skin. As I get older, things like that seem to matter more. This is my way of saying sorry, and making sure that Lex won't want to kill me.'

I wasn't sure I believed any of that. Murray sounded completely sincere, but that's a confidence trickster's stock in trade. Still, it wasn't as if we had any other way of getting to Coldheart.

'Give me a minute,' I said. 'My crew and I need to discuss this before we commit ourselves.'

'Of course,' said Murray. He rose to his feet and moved off a little way to have a quiet conversation with his mirror. The rest of us leaned forward on the plastic chairs and put our heads together.

Annie looked at me steadily. 'Tell me you've got some kind of plan in mind, Gideon.'

'Just the basics,' I said. 'Murray gets us into the maze, Lex deals with the guards, you and I take care of the defences, and Polly uses her tracking skills to guide us to the centre. We grab Sally and the rock, and anything else we like the look of – just to make it clear that no one messes with us and gets away with it – and then we get the hell out of Dodge.'

'Seattle,' said Polly. And then seemed honestly surprised when we all looked at her.

'After I've killed Coldheart,' said Lex.

'We may not have time for that,' I said carefully.

'Then we make time,' said Lex. 'Coldheart has to die for what he's done, or there will always be someone coming after Sally to get at me.'

'We're thieves, not killers,' I said.

'Speak for yourself,' said Lex.

I looked at Annie and Polly. 'Down to you. Are we in?'

They both nodded. We all got to our feet, and Murray turned away from Albert to face us.

'We'll do it,' I said.

Murray smiled happily. 'I knew you would.'

'How are we going to get to Seattle?' said Annie. 'We can't use any of the usual unusual routes. Coldheart will have his people watching them. The only advantage we have is that they don't know we're coming.'

'Fredric Hammer knew all about us,' I said, 'and we still brought him down.'

'Yes . . . what did you do to him?' said Murray. 'He's been acting very strangely just recently.'

'We changed his mind,' I said. 'What unexpected and underhanded method of transport do you have in mind, to smuggle us into Seattle? Would I be right in thinking it involves Albert?'

'Albert's good,' said Murray, patting the mirror's frame

fondly. 'Even better than your Sidney. But neither of them could open a direct path through Coldheart's defences.'

'So how do we do this?' said Polly.

Murray kept his gaze fixed on me, as the one he knew he had to convince. 'I have found you a way in, but you're probably not going to like it.'

'Department of no surprise,' I said. 'Spell it out, Murray.'

'I can use Albert to open a door on to the Low Road.'

'OK . . .' said Polly. 'Why is everybody looking so upset?'

'The Low Road is the path the dead use, to take them from this world to the next,' I said. 'A road so dangerous you have to be dead just to survive it.'

Polly thought about it. 'You know what? I want to go home.'

'You wanted to fight alongside me,' said Lex. 'And that means facing real challenges.' He smiled suddenly. 'Come on, Polly, it'll be fun.'

She smiled back at him. 'Promise?'

'Albert can put you on the Low Road,' said Murray, still keeping his gaze fixed on me, 'but you'll have to rely on Polly's tracking skills to find an exit that will lead you to Seattle's undercity.'

I looked at Polly. 'You think you could do that?'

'How would I know?' said Polly. She looked at Lex. 'But I'll give it my best shot.'

'Good enough,' I said. 'Gather up your courage and fuel-inject your self-preservation instincts, people. We're going.'

SIX

From the Afterlife to the Undercity

The mirror delivered us into the midst of a great open wasteland. It was bitterly cold, with no sign of shelter anywhere. Our breath steamed on the still air, and we all hugged ourselves tightly to keep out the cold. No matter which direction I looked in, we were utterly alone. Nothing moved, and there wasn't a sound anywhere. There might have been buildings once, but they had collapsed long ago. Now it was all churned-up earth and dried mud, with bricks and stones protruding here and there.

As though civilization had come and gone, and left nothing behind but the rubble of our dreams.

'Is this the Low Road?' Polly said finally.

'No,' I said, 'it isn't.'

Annie looked at me. 'How do you know what the Low Road looks like?'

'Because I've been there,' I said.

They all looked at me.

'When was that?' said Annie.

'After Fredric Hammer destroyed our lives,' I said, 'and the protection I bought from Honest John turned out to be worthless, I needed somewhere to hide where Hammer and his people couldn't find me. So I reached out to Sandra Ransom . . .'

'Hold the boat and drop the anchor!' said Polly. 'You know the Divine Busybody? Damn . . . Maybe you are cool, after all.'

'I didn't realize you and Sandra were so close,' said Annie. 'Why is a living goddess so interested in someone like you?'

'One of these days, I'll have to ask her,' I said. 'But now you know why I was so reluctant to ask her for help. I already owe her far too much. The point is, Sandra opened a door for me on to the Low Road, and I stayed there until it was safe for me to come out again.'

'You can stay on the Low Road?' said Annie. 'But that's just for the dead, isn't it?'

'Not always,' I said.

'What was it like?' said Lex. 'In the land of the dead?'

'The Low Road is the path the dead walk, to get to what comes next,' I said. 'It's not meant for living eyes.'

'I thought you didn't seem too pleased at the idea of going back,' said Annie.

'I'm not,' I said. 'I had to work really hard to forget most of what I saw in that place.'

'Why?' said Annie. 'What's so bad about it?'

'You'll have to see for yourself,' I said. 'It's not something you can talk about. It has to be experienced.'

'It is worse than this?' said Polly, glowering at the deserted wasteland. 'Because this is pretty bad.'

'Have you looked at the sky?' said Lex.

We all looked up. The sky was unrelentingly grey, as though made up of endless clouds of dust, and the sun was just a pale-yellow ball, dull and distant.

'A dead sky, for a dead world,' I said.

Polly growled, deep in her throat. 'I'm not hearing any birds or insects . . . And I'm not picking up the scent of a single living thing, apart from us.' She scowled at me accusingly. 'You promised me action and adventure, but this is just . . . nothing!'

'Sometimes the hardest thing to fight is the enemy you can't see,' I said.

Annie frowned. 'You think we're in danger?'

'Feels like it,' I said.

'What from?' Polly said loudly. 'There's nothing here!'

'If this is a dead place,' I said, 'what killed it?'

They all took a moment to think about that.

Polly scowled. 'I'm not smelling any trace of blood or death.'

'But what are your instincts telling you?' said Lex.

Polly turned slowly in a complete circle, ignoring us as she concentrated on our surroundings. When she finally spoke, her voice was low and cautious.

'It feels like we're being watched. But there's no one else here. I'd know.'

Annie looked at me steadily. 'What are we doing in a place like this, Gideon? Could Murray have dumped us here?'

'Why would he want to do that?' I said.

'You tell me,' said Annie. 'He's your friend.'

'Wait and see,' I said. 'Murray doesn't do anything without a reason.'

Annie subsided but didn't look any happier. 'You know I hate it when I can't see a way out of somewhere.'

'I still have my compass,' I said.

Annie sniffed loudly. 'Pardon me if I don't share your confidence. I wouldn't trust that thing to point to a bowl full of porridge in a cottage full of bears.'

'Murray wouldn't just abandon us,' I said.

'How can you be so confident?' said Polly. 'You've already said you don't trust the man.'

'He wouldn't betray us, because he knows me and he knows Lex,' I said. 'He knows we would find our way back to him, whatever it took, and make him pay. Murray is many things, but stupid isn't one of them.'

I broke off as the sky suddenly darkened and night fell like a theatre curtain. The pale sun was gone, replaced by a full moon. Alone in the night sky, with no stars anywhere, its light was dim and lifeless, falling on the empty world like a grey blanket, heavy and smothering. Polly stirred uneasily.

'OK . . . I really don't like the feel of that. It's not natural.'

'I would have thought a full moon would make life easier for you,' said Annie.

Polly looked at her condescendingly. 'Any time is wolf time. It's all about letting the beast out when it wants to play. I can change whenever I feel like it, and I do. Moonlight is good for running in and chasing down your prey, but this light feels . . . wrong.'

Annie glared around her. 'Where the hell is Albert?'

'I don't think he wanted to stick around after he dropped us off,' I said.

'Why didn't you keep an eye on him?' said Annie.

I felt like saying, *Why didn't you?* but I had more sense.

'That's the problem with magical objects that think they're alive,' said Lex. 'They feel obligated to prove they still have free will.'

Annie shot me a hard look. 'Try calling Albert. He might just be waiting for us to summon him.'

That didn't feel particularly likely, but to keep the peace I raised my voice, asking Albert to come and get us. My words fell strangely flat on the quiet, with no trace of an echo. I tried again, but there was still no response.

'Try Sidney,' said Annie. 'He might be able to hear us, now Murray isn't around.'

I called to Sidney, but he didn't answer either.

'Try again,' said Annie. Her mouth was pinched, and her voice sounded strained.

'I don't think that would be a good idea,' I said. 'Too much noise might attract attention.'

'From what?' said Polly, glaring about her. 'I keep telling you: there's nobody else here!'

'But something is watching us,' I said.

'Well, yes, but . . .' said Polly, before stumbling to a halt.

'I don't know what it is that's out there,' I said, 'but I'm really not in any hurry to find out the hard way.'

Polly tried to look in all directions at once and growled again in frustration, a harsh and threatening sound.

'If anything wants to come out and play, I am ready to jump all over it and ruin its day. We'll see whose teeth are bigger . . .'

'Murray must have sent us here for a reason,' I said.

Annie sniffed loudly. 'You say that like it's a good thing. What if he has his own agenda?'

'Well, of course Murray has an agenda,' I said. 'He's a con man.'

'Now you tell us,' said Polly. 'Explain to me again why we should trust this overdressed creep, because right now I feel like taking a big bite out of his buttocks the next time I meet him.'

'He's my friend,' I said.

'Even though you don't approve of him and can't trust him,' said Annie.

'We started out together,' I said. 'A long time ago, when we were both different people. He'd been around even then, and I learned a lot from him. There's more to the man than you might think. Don't judge him too harshly; Murray has always been one of the more abrasive of his personalities.'

'All these people he can be,' said Annie. 'Are they separate identities or just different aspects of the core personality?'

'Beats the hell out of me,' I said. 'I have a hard enough time understanding you.'

'I am large,' Annie said grandly. 'I contain multitudes. And I have a different dress for all of them.'

'I'd still like a straight answer as to whether or not we can trust this Murray,' said Polly.

'He said he'd help us,' I said. 'But I must admit, I'm having a hard time seeing what Murray is getting out of this.'

'Not being killed by the Damned strikes me as a pretty good motivation,' said Annie.

I looked across at Lex, who was staring at the empty horizon. 'Lex only kills people who need killing.'

'What about all the men and women he slaughtered at the Murder Bureau?' said Annie. 'How many of them were merely defending their territory or just in terror for their lives?'

'They were all professional murderers,' I said.

'And that makes Lex the good guy? Because he kills for hate, not money?'

'I don't believe he would kill Murray without a good reason,' I said. 'He's come a long way from the kind of man he used to be.'

'But a lot of that was down to Sally,' said Lex, without looking round. 'And she isn't here any more. I don't know what I'll do if I lose her. I don't know what I'd be. Just damned, I suppose.'

We all looked at him as he stood scanning the horizon for some sign of an enemy, or at least something he could hit. He ignored the cold as though he didn't feel it, and perhaps he didn't. Because he was colder inside than the air could ever be. Polly turned suddenly to scowl at me.

'There's nothing here! Nothing to do, and nothing to do it to! You promised me excitement and adventure!'

'When we get to where we're going, you'll get all of that and more,' I said.

Polly sat down hard on the bare earth and hugged her knees to her chest to try to stop herself shivering. She glared mutinously about her.

'There's not even a cat to chase.'

'What would you do if you caught one?' said Annie.

Polly grinned suddenly. 'Crunchy . . .'

Annie made a point of turning her back on Polly as she talked to me. 'I don't see why we had to rely on Murray for transport in the first place. Why couldn't we take the Midnight Express to Seattle? That got us to Vegas.'

'I was thinking that as well,' said Lex, still not looking round.

'Hold the phone and hit redial,' said Polly, suddenly taking an interest in things again. 'You've travelled on the Midnight Express train? I thought that was just an urban myth!'

'It is,' I said. 'But that doesn't mean it isn't real.'

'What was it like?' Polly said eagerly.

'Eventful,' said Lex.

'Which is one of the reasons I decided not to use it,' I said. 'I think we outstayed our welcome on the previous trip. And while the Midnight Express could almost certainly get us to Seattle, I'm not convinced it could get us into the city under the city. Let alone drop us off inside Coldheart's heavily protected maze. We have to do this Murray's way, because he's the only one who understands what we're going up against.'

'He does seem to know an awful lot,' said Annie. 'For a low-rent confidence trickster. Where is he getting all this information from?'

'I've been thinking about that,' I said. 'Murray knew things I should have known but didn't. I know all kinds of collectors and dealers in the weird and wonderful, but not one of them has ever mentioned Coldheart.'

'You only know those people because you stole the original Gideon's little black book,' Annie said sweetly.

'It's what he would have wanted,' I said.

Polly's ears pricked up. 'The *original* Gideon Sable . . . So you're not him?'

'I am now,' I said. 'I stole his identity, his legend and his life.'

'Of course you did,' said Polly.

'The point is,' I said, just a bit sharply, 'this kind of information comes with the territory when you're a master thief. But not for a small-time hustler like Murray. Who is supposed to be keeping his head down and avoiding people like us, so his many enemies won't be able to find him. No . . . something's wrong with this whole setup. I should have known about a major collector like Coldheart, and it bothers me that I didn't.'

'And I should have heard about Cleopatra Bones and a Mime Called Malice,' said Lex, finally turning his head to look at us. 'I always make it a point to keep up on the competition. So I can be ready, for when someone sends them after me.'

Annie looked at me. 'You said Murray has powers. Maybe that's how he picked up the information.'

'He hasn't dared use his abilities for years,' I said. 'It would be like shining a spotlight in the dead of night. His enemies would be all over him in a moment.'

Polly shrugged, the movement exaggerated by her shivers. 'If Coldheart really is a Howard Hughes hermit, he could simply have put a lot of effort into staying under the supernatural radar. And that's why no one's heard of him.'

'But Murray was quite certain that other collectors had already sent people into the maze,' I said. 'For revenge or the treasure. Which means they have to know about Coldheart. So why hasn't anyone been talking?'

'Because they're afraid?' said Annie.

'And what about all the agents who were sent into the labyrinth?' I said. 'They would have been people like us. We would have known them, or known about them, and we would definitely have noticed if they'd gone missing.'

'You can't know everything,' said Annie.

'This is my area of expertise,' I said. 'Not Murray's.'

'Maybe you're just slipping,' said Polly. 'Getting old.' She scratched her ribs unselfconsciously, as she tried to find a more comfortable patch of bare ground to sit on.

'Remind me to buy you a nice flea collar when we get back,' I said. 'No . . . something is going on, and I'm missing it.'

'What kind of something?' said Annie.

I flashed her a smile. 'Oh, the usual. Hidden motivations, plans within plans, really bad things we won't see coming until the last minute.'

'How can you be so sure?' said Annie.

'Because that's how I'd play it,' I said. I looked around me, taking my time. 'There's something wrong about this place. It feels . . . unfinished.'

Polly suddenly scrambled up on to her feet. 'Something's coming! I can feel it!'

A standing mirror suddenly appeared before us. Polly dropped into a fighting crouch. Lex moved quickly forward to stand at her side.

'Is that Albert or Sidney?' Annie said quietly.

'Albert,' I said.

'How can you be sure?'

'Because they have very different personalities,' I said. 'Besides, Albert is the one with the shabby frame.'

'I heard that!' the mirror said loudly. 'It's a style thing!'

'Where have you been?' I said.

'It's not easy, sir,' said Albert. 'Surfing interdimensional waters. Sometimes you have to wait ages for the tide to flow in the right direction. I blame the subterraneans.'

Annie looked at me. 'Did you understand any of that?'

'Not a word,' I said. 'But I knew Murray wouldn't just dump us here.'

'If you really believed that,' said Lex, 'you wouldn't be looking so relieved.'

Our reflection in the mirror suddenly disappeared, to show Murray smiling out at us. 'Sorry to keep you waiting,' he said. 'It took longer than I anticipated to set things in motion.'

Annie glared at him, not even trying to hide her suspicions. 'Why are we here, and not on the Low Road? And where is this, anyway?'

'You are currently existing inside a dream,' said Murray. 'The kind of nightmare a city has, in the early hours of the morning.'

'OK . . .' said Polly. 'That is not an answer I was expecting. Cities dream? I didn't even know they slept.'

'You must have noticed the difference in how a city feels during the day and at night,' said Murray.

'We're inside a dream?' said Annie.

'Yes!' said Murray. 'And don't think it was easy getting you in here!'

Annie looked at me. 'You said this place didn't feel right.'

'Yes,' I said. 'I did say that, didn't I?' I fixed my gaze on the mirror. 'Why are we here, Murray? What purpose does this serve?'

'You always were the practical one, Gideon,' said Murray. 'I chose this particular location because it's outside reality. While you're here, no one can see or hear you, or pick up on what we're planning to do. You know as well as I do, Gideon, that entrance to the Low Road by the living is strictly forbidden. Doesn't stop people doing it, but it does mean you can't just waltz in.'

'But why have we been kept hanging around here for so long?' said Annie, trying to keep him from seeing how hard she was shivering.

'I needed to let you soak yourselves in this in-between place, so it could take some of the shine off you,' said Murray. 'So you won't stand out among the dead and be noticed.'

'Noticed?' Polly said immediately. 'Who by?'

'Not so much who as what,' said Murray. He took a quick look around. 'There shouldn't be anything inside a city's dream, but you've all felt something, haven't you?'

'Yes,' I said. 'What is it, Murray?'

'Someone has informed Coldheart's people that you're coming for him,' said Murray. 'So they sent something to stop you.'

'What kind of something?' said Lex.

'I don't know,' said Murray. 'But the word is that it's something really unpleasant. I'm sorry, Gideon. I honestly thought

you'd be safe here. But now I have to move you on, before
whatever it is can get a lock on you.'

'Could this thing follow us on to the Low Road?' I said.

'I have no idea,' said Murray. 'Most of the people I talked
to were too scared to even hint at what it might be. And if
they're scared, you should be, too.'

Polly looked at Lex. 'When you offered me a chance to
fight alongside you, I had something more physical in mind.'

'Anything that wants to attack you must take on a material
aspect,' said Lex. 'And that makes it vulnerable to a
material defence.'

Polly grinned. 'Well, that's more like it.'

'Feel free to kick its material arse,' I said. I looked at Murray.
'Can you get us out of this cold now? Before important parts
of our anatomy start dropping off?'

'I have to be careful,' said Murray. 'It's always dangerous,
opening a door into the Low Road. If we get spotted, it could
raise eyebrows in some very elevated places.'

'What are you talking about now?' said Annie.

'What do you think would be set in place to protect the
dead as they head to the hereafter?' I said. 'We're talking
angels and demons. And we really don't want to attract their
attention.'

Lex nodded solemnly. 'That would not be good.'

I stared at him. 'I have always admired your gift for under-
statement. You'd better tuck your halos up your sleeves for
the time being, so their presence won't give us away.'

'They know how to behave in company,' said Lex.

Polly raised a hand, like a child in class. 'Excuse me, but
. . . angels and demons? Are we being metaphorical here?'

'Not even a little bit,' I said.

Polly shrugged. 'It's not my religion.'

'You think they'll care?' said Lex.

Polly realized her hand was still in the air. She brought it
down again and looked unhappily around her.

'Whatever's out there is getting closer. Homing in on us
like a shark that's scented blood in the water.'

I fixed Murray with a hard stare. 'OK, that's it. Get us on
to the Low Road.'

'All right, don't rush me!' Murray peered out from the standing mirror, taking in our surroundings. 'You have no idea how many favours I had to call in to make this work. Take a good look at this face, Gideon, because you won't be seeing it again. I'm going to have to retire Murray the Mentalist for the foreseeable future, and some of me can see a long way into what's coming. I'll have to stick to being other people, hopefully low enough on the food chain that no one knows who they really are. I hope you appreciate what this is costing me, Gideon! I'm only doing this because you're an old friend.'

Lex cut in before I could say anything. 'You're doing this because you put Sally in danger. You are buying your safety by helping us to rescue her.'

'Easy, Lex,' I said. 'Murray is going to send us straight to the Low Road. Isn't that right, Murray?'

'Of course!' he said. 'I can drop you there so gently it won't even make a ripple in the ether. As long as I'm not pressured!'

Lex turned his back on the mirror and walked away. I shot Polly a look, and she hurried after Lex to keep him company. Annie moved in beside me, to give me what support she could. I turned my attention back to Murray.

'Cast your spells or rattle your bones,' I said. 'But get this show on the road right now.'

'I'm doing everything I can for you!' he said sulkily. 'I don't see why I should have to put up with abuse.'

'Lex is the Damned,' I said. 'There was a time when I thought he might not be, but he is now. Don't mess with him.'

'You swore you'd protect me!'

'There's a limit to what I can do.'

Murray looked at me, his gaze cold. 'That is not what I wanted to hear.'

'The sooner you get us to Sally, the sooner I can set about persuading Lex to forget you exist,' I said.

Murray looked at me carefully. 'Are you really so keen to see the Low Road again?'

'You know I'm not,' I said. 'You helped me put my head back together after the first time.'

'That was Osiris,' said Murray. 'She was always quite fond of you. I was never a people person.'

Polly came hurrying back, with Lex close behind her.

'The bad thing has found us!' she said.

She pointed out over the wasteland, and we all turned to look. A deep, dark shadow was sweeping over the horizon and surging across the open ground in a remorseless tide. Like the shadow of something impossibly huge, immersing the world in a nightmare that would never end.

'What the hell has Coldheart sent after us?' said Annie.

'I don't know, and I don't want to find out,' I said. 'Murray! Time to go!'

'Head through the mirror!' said Murray's voice, his image already gone. 'Once you're on the Low Road, trust Polly's tracking instincts to find you a way to Coldheart!'

I glanced back to make sure my crew were behind me, and then I plunged into the mirror. And when we all burst out again, we were in a better place.

The sky blazed with an intense light, as though the sun had expanded to fill the entire horizon. A light so bright should have been overwhelming, but instead it was just a warm illumination that comforted the eye and soothed the soul. And under that magnificent sky, a road went on for ever.

The Low Road was filled to brimming with all kinds of people, from all over the world, from the very old to the very young. A carnival, a festival, or perhaps just a pleasant excursion on a road to somewhere else. Everyone was hurrying along the road, and I could tell it wasn't because they were being driven, or because they were fleeing something behind them; rather, they could sense something wonderful up ahead and they couldn't wait to get to it. All kinds of people, from all kinds of cultures, and all they had in common was a smile. They talked and laughed happily together, but only a vague murmur of sounds reached me. Because they belonged on the Low Road, and I didn't. I was only visiting.

Up ahead, the Low Road branched and split endlessly, offering a wealth of possible destinations. People plunged down side roads without hesitating, as though they had no doubt as to where their choices would lead them. I glanced behind me, but the standing mirror was gone. All I could see was more of the Low Road, and more people heading our way.

Annie looked down and frowned as she took in what we were standing on. 'Am I really seeing a yellow-brick road?'

I nodded solemnly. 'Who says the hereafter doesn't have a sense of humour?'

Annie smiled suddenly and looked up and down the Low Road.

'So many people . . . and all of them happy, laughing, dancing . . .'

'All the dead of all the world,' I said. 'On their way to what comes next.'

'If this is the Low Road,' said Polly, 'and everyone here is dead . . . what have they got to be so cheerful about?'

'All the pains and problems of their lives are finally over,' I said. 'No more fears and worries, no more dreams to let them down or ambitions that will never be fulfilled. Nothing left to vex the spirit or trouble the heart. The worst thing that could possibly happen to them has already happened, and they are set free.'

'Freedom's just another word for nothing left to lose,' said Annie.

I beamed at her. 'Exactly!'

'The road keeps branching off into side routes,' said Lex. 'So many different destinations . . .'

'Heaven and Hell and all points in between,' I said. 'No one is forgotten, and no one gets left out.'

Annie looked at me. 'But if some of these branches lead to Hell, why are people so keen to follow them?'

'Perhaps because Hell isn't what most people think it is,' I said. 'Some say it's just a clearing house, where you can acknowledge your sins and leave them behind.' I looked steadily at Lex. 'Does that sound like something you might recognize?'

He didn't say anything, so I turned back to Annie and Polly.

'I am not a tour guide. Most of what I know about the Low Road came from reading about it afterwards. Trying to make sense of my experiences here.'

'There are books about the Low Road?' said Polly.

'Lots and lots,' I said. 'Most of them completely contradictory.'

'So many different branches,' said Annie. 'What other options are there, apart from Heaven and Hell?'

'God knows,' I said. 'I'm no expert, but I gather the dead can choose to go on or return to the world as someone else or embrace any number of other realities. Life is complicated; why should death be any different?'

'This isn't at all what I thought the Low Road would be like,' said Annie. 'Everyone seems so pleased to be here . . . Why were you so reluctant to come back, Gideon?'

'I put a lot of effort into forgetting this place,' I said, 'because otherwise I wouldn't have been able to think of anything except how to get back here.' I looked steadily at my crew. 'The real danger of the Low Road is that you'll be tempted to stay. To look for everyone you ever lost, all the friends and family who came here before you. To search for heart's ease and trouble's end. And besides . . .'

'Besides what?' said Polly. 'Come on, you can't just stop there.'

'I'm not sure that everything we see here is what it appears to be,' I said. 'No one really understands why the dead have to travel the Low Road, what its purpose is. The only thing I am sure of is that the living have no business being here.'

'Then why are we using this route?' said Polly.

'Because it's the only sure way to bypass Coldheart's protections,' I said. 'By approaching his labyrinth from an entirely unexpected direction.'

'Then let's get going,' said Lex. 'There's nothing here to tempt me.'

I nodded to Polly. 'Jumpstart your tracking skills, follow your instincts and find us an exit ramp to the undercity of Seattle.'

Polly grinned happily and swept the road ahead of us with a challenging gaze. I turned to Annie and Lex.

'Whatever happens, don't get distracted. One step down the wrong branch, and you might not be able to turn back. Not everything that looks heavenly is necessarily somewhere you'd want to spend eternity.'

And then I broke off, as I glanced behind us.

'What is it?' said Annie.

'Something very familiar is following us down the Low Road,' I said slowly.

They all turned to look. A massive shadow was surging along the Low Road, like a stain on the happiest place off earth.

'Is that the same shadow we saw in the city's dream?' said Lex.

'What are the odds there are two really big shadows following us?' I said.

'How the hell did it get here?' said Annie.

'By being a lot more powerful than it has any right to be,' I said. 'Let's get moving, people. And keep your eyes and ears open. The dead and the living aren't the only things that can access the Low Road.'

'Are we talking angels and demons again?' said Polly.

'Among other things,' I said. 'The Hagges are always watching.'

'OK . . .' said Polly. 'Somebody needs a nice sit-down and a cold drink.'

'Just find us the right exit,' I said. 'Before Someone turns up to tell us we shouldn't be here.'

'What kind of Someone?' said Polly.

I looked at her. 'Who do you think?'

Polly sniffed loudly. 'I don't believe in the Great Headmaster in the Sky.'

'Tough,' said Lex. 'He believes in you. And he's a really harsh grader.'

'Hold it,' said Annie, staring thoughtfully at Polly. 'Before we go any further, I want your clothes.'

'What?' said Polly.

'You're going to need your wolf form to properly access your tracking skills,' said Annie. 'Which means you won't need your leathers. But I can't go any further as Annie Anybody. I need to be someone stronger, to get through this.'

'We don't have time for you to create another persona,' I said. 'Just be yourself.'

'No,' said Annie. 'I can't trust me in a crisis.'

'You are seriously weird,' said Polly.

But she was already stepping quickly out of her clothes and dropping them at Annie's feet. The moment she was done with them, Polly covered herself in wolf's fur and stretched luxuriously, showing off her teeth and claws. Annie put on the leather jacket and trousers, the tall boots and black silk scarf, and immediately looked a lot more confident. Her features changed subtly, becoming coarser and more stern, as she wrapped her new identity about her. I'd seen this happen before but still found it unsettling that the woman I loved could so easily be replaced by someone similar but different. As though there were any number of people hanging around inside Annie's head, just waiting to be called forward so they could have their moment in the spotlight.

'Call me Grace,' she said, in a harsh, flat voice.

'Tell me I don't look like that when I'm wearing my leathers,' said Polly.

'Like what?' said Grace.

'A biker chick from Hell,' said Polly.

'I like it,' said Grace. 'It feels very me.'

'Whoever that is,' I murmured.

'Trust me,' said Grace. 'I'm what you need to get us through this.'

Polly just sniffed. 'It will take more than my cast-offs to make you a real fighter.'

Grace smiled slowly. 'I've fought worse things than you in my time.'

'Ladies . . .' I said quickly. 'This isn't the time or the place to be playing *mine are bigger than yours*.'

'She started it!' said Polly.

'She usually does,' I said. 'Please, just concentrate on finding the right exit. Before the shadow catches up with us.'

Polly glanced back at the darkness. It was noticeably closer, and a great many branches had already disappeared inside it, although none of the dead walking the road seemed in the least bothered by its presence. Polly padded forward, and the rest of us hurried after her.

The Low Road stretched off and away, and the dead walked

cheerfully along it. None of them so much as glanced at us, because they had far more important things on their minds. Polly moved faster and faster, drawn on by something, plunging through everyone who got in her way, as though the dead were no more tangible than ghosts. They didn't seem to notice her, but I felt a chill every time I passed through one of them.

The dead were choosing new routes all the time, as though responding to signposts and directions only they could see. And sometimes I saw things that helped me understand why. A small child toddled down the road on its own, to where a mother and father stood waiting with outstretched arms. An old man stumbled down a side road to where an old woman stood waiting, both of them growing younger the closer they got.

I liked the idea that, in the end, everyone gets to go home.

I almost slammed into Lex's back when he stopped abruptly to stare down a side road. Polly just kept on going, intent on what was before her, and I had to yell after her to get her to stop. The werewolf dropped down on to her haunches and looked reluctantly back over her shoulder. I moved in beside Lex, but he didn't even glance at me.

'What is it?' I said quietly.

He gestured at the side road before him.

'I'm not seeing anything, Lex,' I said carefully.

'You don't see that woman?' he said, in a quiet, lost voice. 'She's waiting for me.'

I looked hard, and after a moment it seemed to me that I could see something. Just a dim figure, standing very still, that refused to come into focus. Perhaps because she wasn't there for me. I thought I knew what Lex was going to say.

'It's my wife,' said Lex. 'My first wife, Barbara. The one I damned myself over, trying to bring her back from the dead.'

He started forward. I grabbed hold of his arm, but he just dragged me along with him. I moved quickly to stand in front of him, blocking his way. Lex came to a halt, rather than walk right through me, but he still wouldn't look at me.

'Let her go,' I said.

'But it's my wife!'

'If you love her, let her go,' I said. 'It's not for us – any of this.'

Grace moved in on Lex's other side. 'What about Sally, Lex? Are you going to leave her trapped in the labyrinth, for Coldheart to kill when he grows tired of her? If you go down this road instead . . . We might not be able to save Sally without you.'

Lex hesitated, his gaze fixed on the woman he thought he'd lost for ever.

'Are you even sure you'd be allowed to be with your first wife?' said Grace. 'Or do you believe she's damned to Hell, as well as you?'

I looked at her sharply. Such coldness wasn't like Annie. But it seemed to work with Lex, bringing him out of his daze like a slap to the face. He nodded slowly.

'Sally is my wife now. I'm not even sure Barbara would recognize me, after what I've made myself into. And perhaps . . . I wouldn't want her to see me like this.'

He turned back to the main road and set off again. Grace and I walked with him, trying to support him with our presence. Polly was already on her feet and hurrying forward to take the lead again. Her whole wolf form was quivering with eagerness, as though she'd locked on to a scent.

'I never thought the afterlife would be like this,' Lex said finally.

'There are more branches in the Low Road than any of us can count,' I said. 'Everyone here seems to know where they have to go. Presumably, you will, too, when it's your turn.'

'To Hell,' said Lex.

'Nothing is certain,' said Grace. 'There is always the possibility of mercy.'

'Not for me,' said Lex. 'Not after everything I've done, and will do, to get Sally back. I have waded in blood and soaked myself in slaughter, and I do not regret any of it.' He looked at Polly and raised his voice. 'How much further?'

Polly just kept going. Lex increased his speed, leaving Grace and me behind. We let him go, so he could be alone with his thoughts. And then Grace suddenly stopped, to stare down a side turning. I stopped with her.

'Keep your gaze on the road,' I said kindly. 'There's nothing here you need to see.'

'Is everything here real?' said Grace.

'I believe so,' I said. 'That's what makes it dangerous. And cruel. Life has enough temptations, without death adding more.'

Grace tore her gaze away from whatever she was seeing, so she could look at me.

'How did you survive in this place?'

'I wasn't here long,' I said.

'But you saw things, didn't you?'

'I saw people I would give everything I have to see again,' I said steadily. 'But as Lex said, would they even recognize who I've become? It's better for them that we move on.'

Grace shook her head slowly. 'What we're putting ourselves through . . . just to save Switch It Sally.'

'And to show Coldheart what happens when he messes with us,' I said.

'What price paradise, when there's revenge to be had?' said Grace.

She turned away from whoever was waiting down the side road and set off after Lex and Polly, and I went with her. I didn't glance down any of the side roads we passed, because I knew who would be there. And I couldn't stand to have my heart broken again.

We'd only just caught up with Lex and Polly when the werewolf suddenly crashed to a halt and pointed out a particular side route with a hairy hand. The branch she'd found looked like all the others, except there was no one looking back at us.

'You're sure this is the right way?' I said to Polly.

'It feels right,' said Polly. 'I'm almost certain this is the exit we need.'

'Almost?' said Grace.

'Instincts don't come with a percentage reading.'

'Lead the way, Polly,' I said. 'We don't belong here. We still have work to do.'

She nodded quickly and started down the branch, and we all went after her. I did glance back once, and the huge and terrible shadow seemed a lot closer. I shot it the finger and followed the others out of the Low Road. We left a better place behind, so we could emerge on to an old-fashioned city street.

The warmth and peace of the Low Road disappeared, replaced by the cold, grey aspect of a Victorian street scene. Polly turned back into her human form, shuddered briefly and went werewolf again.

'I don't like this place,' she said. 'All my instincts are screaming at me to get the hell out of here while I still can.'

'Take it easy,' I said. 'Between us, we can handle anything Coldheart and his people can throw at us.'

'You sure about that?' said Polly.

'You want it in writing?' I said.

'So, this is the city underneath Seattle,' Grace said quickly. 'First question . . . Why do all the buildings here seem to be made of wood?'

'That was the problem,' I said. 'The original city harks back to the nineteenth century, when people preferred wood over stone. So when the great fire started in 1899, it reduced most of the city to ashes. What was left wasn't worth preserving, so they built their new city on top of the old.'

'How do you know so much about this?' said Polly.

'I read,' I said. 'If you're going to be a master thief, you need to know things.'

The dusty, grey street had the feel of a place that had been abandoned a long time ago. All the shops and houses had clearly been empty for some time. Doors hung open, as though the owners had just run away and left them. The windows were blank and vacant, like unseeing eyes. Here and there, old-time advertisements offered goods and brands that hadn't been available for generations, at prices that would shock modern sensibilities. There were no lights in any of the buildings, and the lamp-lit street had a cold and desolate feel. The whole scene was oppressively quiet, like a cemetery no one bothered to visit any more.

I looked at Polly. 'Which way?'

She turned her lupine head back and forth, as though

listening to some inner voice, and then stabbed a hairy finger at one particular side street. She started down it, and we all followed after her.

'A deserted labyrinth of sealed-over Victorian streets,' said Grace. 'You take me to the nicest places, Gideon.'

'Think of the treasure house at the end,' I said.

Grace nodded. 'That does help.'

We moved quickly through one empty street after another, keeping a cautious eye on our surroundings. There had to be hidden traps and waiting guards, but so far they were conspicuous by their absence. It was so quiet that all I could hear were the soft ghostly scuffings of our feet on the dusty floor. I tried not to think about the stone ceiling, set a lot lower than I was comfortable with. I tried to visualize the modern city of Seattle above us, but that just made me feel even more as though we were buried in the grave of the old city. Gas street lamps stood at regular intervals, but their weird shimmering glow had nothing to do with gas. It felt more like some strange phosphorescence – a living light in a dead place.

'We're not alone down here,' Grace said quietly.

'Can you see anyone?' I said, just as quietly.

'No,' said Grace. 'But it definitely feels like we're being watched.'

'Hey,' said Polly. 'I do the feelings, in this crew.'

'All right,' I said. 'Do you feel like we're being watched?'

'Oh, sure,' said Polly. 'But I sort of took that for granted.'

'How much further to the centre of the maze?' said Lex.

'Some way yet,' said Polly.

'How far?' said Lex.

Polly shook her head unhappily. 'It's hard to get any sense of distance. Something bad happened here, or was made to happen, to seal off this section of the undercity. We only got in because we came through the Low Road. I'm not sure how we're going to get out again.'

'That's a problem for later,' I said. 'Concentrate on where they're keeping Sally.'

Polly shrugged. 'You do know we're walking into a trap?'

'I sort of took that for granted,' I said. 'In fact, I'm surprised no one's already shooting at us.'

Polly growled and shook her head. 'I can't believe we're putting our lives on the line for Switch It bloody Sally.'

'She has hidden qualities,' Lex said firmly.

'Really well hidden,' said Polly.

'Are you picking up on anything, apart from the watching eyes?' I said.

'Not a thing,' said Polly. 'We're completely alone. Probably because everyone else had the good sense to get out of here.'

'Coldheart must have set traps somewhere,' I said. 'Presided over by a whole lot of guards with really big guns.'

'Because that's what you'd do,' said Grace.

'Exactly,' I said.

'If there were any of those things, I would see or hear or smell them,' said Polly.

'Not if they've been specially trained to deal with people like us,' I said.

'There are no people like us,' said Lex.

'Don't forget Coldheart's security chiefs,' said Grace. 'Cleopatra Bones and a Mime Called Malice.'

'Trust me,' I said. 'I haven't forgotten. Mimes are creepy. Even worse than clowns.'

'There's nothing funny about a clown at midnight,' said Grace. 'Especially if he's got an erection.'

Polly snorted briefly with laughter.

'And I really don't like heading into unknown territory without a plan,' I said.

'Who needs a plan when you've got my instincts to guide you?' said Polly. 'I can feel the centre up ahead. Like it's calling to me.'

'And we should, of course, trust this voice you're hearing in your head,' said Grace. 'And carry on rushing blindly into danger.'

'You've turned very abrasive since you put on the leathers,' I said.

'Comes with the persona,' said Grace.

Polly shook her head. 'Weird upon weird . . .'

'I'm not the one who's leading us into a trap,' said Grace.

'We have to go on,' I said. 'Lex needs to rescue Sally; you and I need to get our rock back, and a chance to stick it to Coldheart in the process; and Polly needs adventure and something to hit. And probably bite. There's bait in this trap for all of us.'

'You bait a trap to bring the prey to the killing ground,' said Lex.

'You're thinking about the minotaur, aren't you?' said Grace.

'Aren't you?' I said.

Grace cracked her knuckles. 'Bring it on. I could use something to take out my frustrations on.'

'Damn right!' said Polly.

'No,' said Lex. 'You leave the minotaur to me.'

'Why?' said Polly, bristling. 'I have strength and speed, teeth and claws.'

'I am armoured by Heaven and Hell,' said Lex.

'OK . . .' said Polly. 'You're the Damned.'

Lex smiled briefly. 'Set one monster to kill another.'

'You're not a monster, Lex,' I said.

'I will be,' he said. 'If that's what it takes to save Sally.'

SEVEN
Time See What's Become of Me

The unnatural light from the street lamps didn't travel far, and the shadows seemed to be growing deeper and darker. I kept a careful eye on them as my crew and I headed deeper into the undercity. I still couldn't see any signs of traps or guards, and the only sounds came from my crew's footsteps. There was nothing to suggest anyone had walked the abandoned streets of the undercity for a very long time.

Normally, I made a point of taking the lead when my crew was working, because I was the man with the plan, and therefore the only one who knew what was really going on. But because I didn't have anything like a plan this time, I let Polly take point, so she could follow her nose and her instincts. She padded tirelessly along the narrow streets, as though following signs and directions only she could see.

Polly kept to her werewolf form, perhaps because she felt safer that way in unknown territory. The claws on her paws clicked regularly against the ground like a metronome, ticking off the time it was taking us to get to the centre of the maze. After a while, she started pausing at every crossroads or intersection, raising her head to sniff at the air before moving off again. I was starting to wonder whether Coldheart and his people could have packed up and moved on. Just because Murray said they were still here didn't make it a fact. Murray had been wrong before. I had been there with him when it happened and had helped haul his arse out of the line of fire afterwards. I would have felt better if the information had come from Madam Osiris. I trusted her; at least, I trusted her more than I trusted Murray.

I suddenly realized we'd come to a halt and hadn't started moving again. Polly was crouched down on her haunches in the middle of the street, her fur bristling. I actually felt a little relieved that we'd finally come up against something dangerous. It made our presence here feel less like a wild goose chase. We all took a good look around, straining our eyes against the uncertain light, but there didn't seem to be anything out there. When Polly still didn't say anything, I moved in beside her.

'Speak to me, Polly,' I said quietly. 'What's spooking you?'

She shook her head slowly, not taking her eyes off the street ahead. 'I don't know. It's just a feeling. Probably nothing.'

'Then we need to move on,' I said. 'Standing around in the open makes us targets.'

I didn't like how impatient Lex was getting, now we were finally close to rescuing Sally. I only had to glance at the Damned to see the tension rising in him. The only reason he hadn't already stormed off and left us behind was that he needed Polly's tracking skills to take him to Sally.

I said Polly's name again, more sharply, and she growled under her breath before reluctantly padding forward. We all fell in behind her, sticking close. I checked out every side street we passed, without being too obvious about it. If Polly had a bad feeling, so did I. There had to be traps and guards somewhere; if I'd been Coldheart, I would have surrounded my treasure house with all the protections money could buy. There's nothing like having valuable things to make some people determined to take them away from you. Often by sending someone like me and my crew.

I glanced at Grace, striding along beside me and apparently entirely unconcerned by our surroundings. She seemed much more confident since she put on Polly's leathers. Usually, Annie carefully constructed each of her characters, detailing every part of their individual back story, before bringing them to life through the expert use of clothes and wigs and makeup. But this time Annie had been forced to build a new persona from very little in the way of props. I wasn't sure whether I should be impressed or worried by her achievement. I'd been trying to persuade Annie that she didn't need to rely so much on her other personalities; that she could do anything she needed as Annie, without having to take on some more special-ized personality. But in times of stress, she always resorted to her old ways.

She caught me looking at her and smiled briefly. 'How does it feel? To be walking into danger without a properly prepared plan?'

'Exhilarating!' I said briskly. 'I should do this more often.'

'You're not fooling anyone but yourself,' said Grace. 'Tell me you at least have something worked out for when we get to where we're going.'

'Not really,' I said. 'I'm putting all my money on improvising wildly and hoping for the best. Though I have been thinking . . .'

'I know,' said Grace. 'I've seen you scowling. If you are about to tell me that not everything in this heist is necessarily what it seems, I am a country mile and a half ahead of you.'

'I might have an idea or two as to what's really going on in the background,' I said.

'And?'

'I'm still thinking,' I said. 'I could be wrong. In fact, part of me hopes I am.'

'But if it should turn out that you're right,' Grace said carefully, 'do you have a plan on how to deal with it?'

'Well . . .' I said. 'Not so much a plan as a last resort that could just as easily make things worse instead of better.'

Grace sighed loudly. 'And you're not going to tell me anything about this possible last resort, because you know I wouldn't approve.'

I beamed at her. 'Exactly!'

'You really are going to have to learn to trust me, Gideon.'

'Trust who?' I said.

Instead of answering me, Grace stared at the street stretching away before us. The empty buildings stared back like so many tombstones, dead remnants of a dead city. We'd been walking for some time, and only the details on the shopfronts had changed.

'These boots are killing me,' said Grace. 'For a werewolf, Polly has surprisingly small feet. When are we going to enter the labyrinth?'

'I think we're already in it,' I said. 'The streets of the undercity make up the maze, with the treasure house at its centre. Good thing we brought Polly, or we wouldn't have had a hope in hell of finding our way.'

The werewolf stopped again, sitting down hard enough to raise a small cloud of dust. She sneezed absently and stared fiercely around. Her hackles were standing up. I moved in beside her, hoping I could steady her with my presence.

'What's the problem?' I said quietly.

'I can sense the centre up ahead,' she said quietly. 'But I can't seem to work out how to get there. Ever since we arrived, it feels like we've been set adrift in Space and Time. I don't think we're underneath the actual city of Seattle, but rather walking through some separate pocket dimension. Lost in the fabric of reality . . .'

'Wonderful,' said Grace. 'A philosophical werewolf. Just what we need.'

I shot her a reproachful look. 'Please don't taunt the scary pissed-off werewolf woman.'

Polly grinned widely at Grace, showing her teeth. 'Yeah, pipe down or I'll take my leathers back.' And then she rose up suddenly, six feet and more of lean, powerful wolf, her muscles taut and straining, as though she was getting ready to launch herself at some unseen enemy. 'Did you hear that?' she said softly. 'Someone is heading our way.'

'Human?' I said.

'If it is,' said Polly, 'they smell really rank.'

'Could it be the minotaur?' said Lex.

Grace smiled and cracked her knuckles loudly enough to make everyone wince. 'Bring it on. I am definitely in the mood to punch someone with a bull's head.'

'We don't know it's an enemy,' I said.

'We don't know that it isn't,' said Lex.

'What else could it be?' said Grace. 'It's not like we have any friends down here.'

'And whatever it turns out to be, we can't give it a chance to sound the alarm,' said Lex.

'There's something really off about it,' said Polly.

Her head snapped around, and she fixed her gaze on one particular side alley. And from out of the shadows came an old man, stumbling and uncertain on his feet. He stopped abruptly and stared at us with wide, shocked eyes. He had long white hair and a straggly white beard, and what we could see of his face was a mass of wrinkles. A hunched, emaciated figure, his clothes were ragged and faded, and his shoes had all but fallen apart. He lurched forward again, heading straight for us on tottering legs, his arms stretched out – either to welcome us or because he needed to reassure himself we were real. Tears streamed down his shrunken cheeks.

'People,' he said. 'It's been so long . . . since I saw people.'

His voice was rough and harsh, as though he hadn't used it for a long time. He collapsed before he could reach us, sitting down suddenly in the middle of the street, as though all the strength in his legs had run out. I looked quickly at Lex and Polly.

'You two stay here and keep an eye on our surroundings. This could be a distraction, while the real threat comes from somewhere else.'

They nodded sharply and moved to stand back to back, so they could keep a watch on all the side streets. I turned to Grace.

'Want to help me talk to old Ben Gunn?'

'Love to,' said Grace.

We approached the aged figure cautiously, and he smiled at us through his tears. He looked too worn out and used up to offer any kind of threat, but I wasn't in the mood to take chances. It wasn't until I saw the old man up close that I realized his condition was simply too sad to be anything but real. He looked as though he hadn't eaten properly in ages, and he was so pitifully grateful to see us he couldn't get any words out past the tears. Grace and I knelt down before him, and he reached out to pat our faces softly with his wrinkled hands, just to make sure we were real and solid. He laughed breathlessly, and the tears finally stopped.

'So many years,' he said, 'since I saw anyone . . . talked to anyone.'

'Can you tell us your name?' I said.

'Michael Sharpe,' he said slowly. 'Gentleman thief and burglar to the trade. That's why she sent me here, because I was the best . . .'

I frowned. It seemed to me I recognized that name, from not long ago. Sharpe peered down at his ragged clothes.

'Look at the state of me . . . I was always so well dressed. I used to boast I could be invited anywhere and still fit in.'

'How did you get here?' said Grace.

'Judi Rifkin sent me,' said Sharpe. 'She said it would be simple – easy in and easy out. But once I was here, I couldn't find the treasure house and I couldn't find any way out.'

'How long have you been here?' I said.

'For ever,' said Sharpe. 'I don't eat or drink or sleep. All I do is wander the streets. Sometimes I see things, horrible things . . .' He looked around him, his face full of fear. 'I don't talk to the bad things.'

He tugged absently at his beard, and then held his hands up and studied them with something like shock, as though he couldn't believe such withered things could be his.

'Trapped,' he said. 'Like a rat in a maze. And now you're here, you're trapped as well. There's no way out.'

'You never found Coldheart's treasure house?' I asked.

'I never found anything,' he said.

'What about the minotaur?' said Grace.

He looked at her blankly. 'There isn't another living being anywhere in this place. I've been so alone. In the cold and the dark.' He peered carefully around him, and then lowered his voice. 'But you need to beware of the dead.'

I waited for more, but he just sat there, looking around and muttering to himself.

'Judi Rifkin sent you?' I said, prompting him.

He nodded hard, as though this was one of the few things he was still sure of. 'She had to bring in a specialist. This spooky old lady in a tweed suit, who giggled a lot. She drew a chalk circle on the floor, pushed me inside it and snapped her fingers and, just like that, I was here. Judi promised me there would be all kinds of exits, but she lied. She lied . . .'

His head dropped forward, as though just talking had worn him out. I looked at Grace.

'He can't have been here long,' I said. 'Not if he worked for Judi Rifkin. She's only been operating on her own for a few years.'

Grace tapped Sharpe gently on the shoulder, and his head came up again. He smiled at her like a trusting child.

'How old were you when you came here?' said Grace.

'I was twenty-five,' said the old man. 'I had my whole life in front of me.'

His head dropped forward again, until his chin hit his chest, and after a moment I realized he'd stopped breathing. I tried for a pulse in his neck but couldn't find one.

'He finally got out,' I said.

I laid the old man on his back, crossed his hands on his chest and stood up. Grace moved in beside me.

'This didn't just happen,' I said. 'Someone did this to him.'

'Then we'd better find out who,' said Grace. 'Before they do it to us.'

Lex and Polly came over to stand with us.

'Did he have anything useful to say?' said Lex.

Grace was still looking at the old man. 'Just *beware of the dead.*'

Polly frowned. 'What does that mean?'

'I'm sure we'll find out,' I said.

Lex turned to Polly. 'Can you still sense where the centre is?'

The werewolf looked at the street ahead of her. 'It's not far now. But it's so hard to pin down . . . I'm not sure I can get you there.'

'Of course you can,' said Lex. 'I have faith in you.'

Polly met his gaze steadily. 'Why?'

Lex smiled briefly. 'Because you're the infamous Polly Perkins. You track like I kill.'

She grinned back at him. 'Now that's what I call a compliment.'

She set off down the street, sniffing hard at the still air, and then shot off down a side street. The rest of us followed after her.

A few streets later, we stopped again as we saw a mummy sitting on the sidewalk, its back pressed against a street lamp. Not the bandaged kind, but a human body that had dried out and shrunk in on itself. It was wearing faded clothes and looked as though it had been dead for a very long time.

'He looks like he just sat down when he got too tired to go on,' I said. 'After he died, the undercity's air and humidity must have done the rest.'

'Like the old man,' said Grace. 'Only more so. What the hell is going on here?'

I looked at Polly. 'You didn't smell this?'

'That body's been here so long it smells like everything else,' Polly said defensively. 'Like dust!'

'Maybe it's a warning,' said Grace. 'Go back while you still can.'

Lex shook his head immediately. 'Not going to happen. We came here to save Sally.'

'If she's still here,' said Polly.

'She's here,' said Lex. 'She has to be.'

'Check all the side streets, people,' I said. 'This could be a distraction.'

'Stop saying that!' said Polly. 'There's no one else here!'

'Coldheart's people didn't just leave this mummy sitting around because they're not very house-proud,' I said. 'Grace is right; this is a warning. And a threat.'

The others indulged me with a good look around, but even after they'd peered down all the side streets, there wasn't a trace of an enemy anywhere. We finally came together again to take another good look at the mummy. Lex stirred impatiently.

'We need to press on and find Sally. What's so important about a dried-up corpse?'

I shot him a hard glance. 'The old man said, *beware of the dead*. And this looks pretty dead to me.'

I leaned in close for a better look. Only a few whisps of hair remained attached to the mummy's skull, and the skin on the face had been stretched so taut that all vestiges of humanity had disappeared. The eyes had sunk back into their sockets, and blackened lips had pulled back from the teeth, leaving the mouth gaping in a scream that would never end.

I searched carefully through the mummy's pockets until I found a wallet with a driving licence.

'Sal Brenchley,' I said. 'I remember him. Freelance muscle, mostly for the Terrible Twins. He disappeared a few years back.'

'How could he end up like that after only a few years?'
said Grace.

'This isn't any natural phenomenon,' I said. 'This was enemy
action, designed to discourage those who came after him.'

Grace scowled at the mummy. 'And I was worried about a
minotaur . . .'

'Maybe you should have brought a big red cape,' I said.

I slipped the wallet back into the mummy's top pocket.
'Sorry, Sal.'

'Never heard of him,' said Polly. 'Or the people he worked
for.'

'The Twins used to be big-time operators in the collecting
game,' said Grace. 'Until some really important deals collapsed.
Sending Sal to burgle Coldheart's treasure house must have
been their last gamble.'

'But he got trapped in here, just like Michael Sharpe,' I said.

'Murray said lots of agents were sent in here,' said Grace.
'So what happened to all the others?'

'Never mind that,' said Polly. 'Look at the state of that
thing! Is this going to happen to us?'

'Not as long as we remember to moisturize,' I said.

'Funny,' said Polly. 'Funny man.'

Grace gestured for me to step to one side, so we could talk
privately.

'Even if we do find our way to the centre,' she said quietly,
'and break into the treasure house, and rescue Sally, and get
our rock back . . . how are we going to get out of here?'

'There has to be an exit somewhere,' I said confidently.
'Coldheart might be happy playing hermit, but his security
chiefs must be able to come and go, because they went to
Paris to kidnap Sally and bring her back here. So all we have
to do is find Cleopatra Bones and the Mime, and ask them
how they did that.'

'What if they don't feel like telling us?' said Grace.

I smiled. 'Then we give them to Lex.'

Grace nodded solemnly. 'That should do it. Thank you,
Gideon. I feel a bit better, now I know there has to be an exit
somewhere. And it's good to know you're still the man with
the plan.'

'Always,' I said.

Polly made a loud startled sound, and we looked quickly round to see her backing away from the mummy as it slowly turned its head. The eyelids opened, revealing a gaze full of hate and hunger, and then the mouth stretched wide to let out a howl of inhuman fury. The sound didn't echo on the still air and soon died away, as though there wasn't enough air in the lungs to keep it going. In the sudden hush, I could hear the patter of approaching footsteps. I gestured for the crew to stand together, and we quickly took up positions so we could look in every direction at once. More mummies started to appear, shrivelled-up things with the faces of preserved corpses, lurching and stumbling out of the shadows and into the light. And every single one of them headed straight for us, their faces full of an endless fury.

Beware of the dead . . .

Grace hunched her shoulders inside her black leather jacket and clenched her hands into fists. 'What the hell are those things?'

'An answer to your question,' I said. 'What happened to all the agents sent in to loot Coldheart's treasure house? None of them found it, and none of them got out. They died here and ended up as guard dogs, protecting the place they'd come to rob. Someone here takes their irony straight. I was wondering why we hadn't walked into any guards or traps. This is the trap, and these are the guards.'

The halos at Lex's wrists blazed fiercely as the angelic armour swept over him, enveloping him from head to foot behind an impenetrable shield, cutting him off from all human weakness. The light blazing from one side of his armour was fierce enough to illuminate the whole street, and the dark side was deeper than any of the surrounding shadows. Polly shrank back from Lex and turned her head away. The sheer presence of the armour was too much for her werewolf senses to cope with. She was part of the natural world, and there was nothing natural about the Damned's armour.

He turned his featureless face to me. 'Any objections if I take first crack at these overly energetic corpses?'

'You go right ahead,' I said. 'I'll stand here and make notes.'

The original mummy had pulled itself up and on to its feet, clinging to the street lamp with both hands. It pushed itself away and lurched towards us. The Damned went to meet it, and the moment he was close enough, the mummy launched itself at him with inhuman speed and force. It hit the Damned hard but couldn't even rock him back on his heels. The mummy lashed out at the Damned, but its clawed fingers just rattled uselessly across his armour. The Damned slammed a fist into the mummy's ribs. Bones broke and splintered, but the mummy didn't give a damn.

It clawed viciously at the Damned, trying to find a weak spot, and even clattered its teeth against his throat, but they just shattered on the armour. The Damned grabbed hold of the mummy with both hands, lifted it easily into the air and threw it to the ground with such force the impact broke all its bones.

The mummy lay there for a moment, not moving, not breathing, and then the broken arms and legs levered the body back on to its feet. The smashed body stood swaying for a moment, and then it forced itself forward, step by step. Driven on by orders that kept it moving long after it should have lain down and given up the ghost. Shards of broken bone pierced its skin, but there was no blood. The Damned went to meet the mummy, while I took a quick look around at all the others closing in on us, from every direction at once. And still more of the withered things emerged from the side streets and alleyways, homing in on us.

Dead bodies, animated by a hatred for the living.

The original mummy raised a clawed hand, and the Damned lost his patience. He tore the withered arm right out of the socket and threw it to one side. The mummy reached out with its other arm, so the Damned ripped that one off, too. The mummy still kept coming, so the Damned tore its head clean off its shoulders. He threw the head to the ground and stamped on it, crushing the skull. The headless, armless body finally stopped moving. The Damned backhanded the thing away from him, and it crashed to the ground and didn't move again.

The Damned looked back at us. 'Remove the head. That seems to do the job.'

'Thanks,' I said. 'We did notice.'

The Damned strode off down the street and right into the midst of the advancing mummies. He lashed out with his armoured fists, doing terrible damage, but the mummies just crowded in around him, grabbed his arms and tried to drag him down through sheer force of numbers. He struck them down with vicious blows, pulled them off him and threw them away, but no matter how much damage he did, there were always more to replace those who fell. The mummies swarmed all over him, clawing and biting, until he was almost lost to view.

Finally, they pulled him down. He crashed on to his back and didn't rise again, held in place by the sheer weight of so many bodies.

The remaining mummies were still heading our way. It only took me a few quick glances to confirm we were surrounded on all sides, with no way out. I started to say something, but Polly got in first.

'They don't look like they've got any silver on them, so they can't do me any real damage. I'll open up a corridor, and then you two should run like hell. I'll rescue Lex, and we'll catch up with you.'

'We could fight the mummies, too,' said Grace.

'But could we win?' I said. I nodded to Polly. 'These things don't look too bright. You keep them busy, and I'll think of something.'

'Of course,' said Polly. 'That's what you do.'

She dropped on to all fours and charged the mummies, crashing through their ranks and sending them flying. She tore out throats with her powerful jaws and gutted mummies with her claws. She hit them hard and danced back out of reach, moving too quickly for the dead to lay a hand on her. But there were so many of them that Polly couldn't keep dodging their reaching hands, and while she might be damaging the mummies, she wasn't stopping them. She followed Lex's lead and started ripping off heads, but the sheer effort involved slowed her down enough that the mummies were able to close in and hit her from every side at once. Clawed hands sank deep into her dark fur, opening terrible wounds, and the werewolf howled miserably as blood flew on the air. The wounds healed quickly, but the mummies tore Polly apart faster than she could put herself back together. They piled on top of the werewolf and dragged her down. She disappeared under a mass of vicious clawing figures, and her howls turned to screams.

There was nothing Grace or I could do for her. And nowhere we could run. Every exit was blocked off by a horde of malevolent blood, while more spilled into the street, filling it up. All Grace and I could do was move quickly over to the side of the street and set our backs against a shop window, so nothing could creep up on us from behind. Grace held her clenched fists out before her and waited for something to come within reach. I thought hard. Grace shot me a quick glance.

'We need a plan, Gideon!'

'I'm working on one!'

'Work faster!'

I had my hand on my time pen, but even if I did stop Time and freeze the mummies where they were, it would be an impossible task to drag so many bodies off Polly and the Damned, against the stubborn resistance of the frozen world. I would run out of strength and breath, long before I accomplished anything. Now that the two most dangerous targets had been taken care of, the remaining mummies were advancing on Grace and me. Taking their time, because they knew we had nowhere left to go. Grace raised her fists defiantly and shot me a determined smile.

'When there's nothing left to do but die, die well.'

'Things aren't that bad. I think those leathers have gone to your head.'

'Do you have a better idea?'

'I'm thinking!'

'Then think faster!' said Grace.

Dead hands smashed through the shop window behind us, showering us with broken glass. We had no choice but to run back into the street and what little open space was left. Grace and I moved quickly to stand back to back. I could feel the tension in her back muscles as she braced herself for the attack, but if the Damned and a werewolf couldn't stop the mummies, I couldn't see us lasting long.

'Use the time pen, Gideon,' said Grace. 'Make a run for it.'

'I wouldn't get far, dragging you with me.'

'Then leave me,' said Grace.

'Not going to happen,' I said. 'And I won't abandon Lex and Polly either.'

'Maybe you could go find us some help.'

'Who from?' I said. 'It's not like we have any friends down here.'

I racked my brains, trying to remember everything I'd ever read about dead men walking and mummified bodies. A common denominator finally came to mind, and I laughed out loud.

'You have a plan!' said Grace. 'Whatever this plan is, I want you to know that I love it and want to have its babies, and you should start it immediately.'

'Mummies are vulnerable to fire!' I said.

There was a slight pause.

'That's it?' said Grace. 'Neither of us smoke, so we don't even have a lighter or matches! Wait a minute, these aren't my clothes . . .'

She started searching quickly through her pockets, but I was already shouting at the pile of mummified bodies covering the Damned.

'Lex! Stop lying down on the job and get your arse out of there! I have a plan to stop this, but I can't do it without you. On your feet, Damned!'

The heap of mummies exploded, with broken bodies flying in all directions as the Damned rose up. Some of the mummies still clung to him, only to fall away as he shook himself like a dog fresh out of the rain. The Damned struck away the last few clinging hands and turned his armoured face in my direction.

'You had better have a really good idea, Gideon.'

'Mummies burn!' I said. 'They're so dry they'll go up like paper!'

'Then it's a shame my armour doesn't come with a built-in flame-thrower,' said the Damned.

'Use the light from the street lamps!' I said. 'Magical fires, to burn magical mummies!'

The Damned strode across the street, slamming mummies out of his way with great sweeps of his arms. He tore a lamp out of the sidewalk and brought the top part slamming down on a mummy's head. The lamp exploded, and shimmering light leaped out and set fire to the mummy's face.

Flames engulfed the shrivelled head and then shot down the body in a roar of burning light. The mummy staggered back and forth, blazing fiercely as flames consumed the dried-up body like firewood. The mummy flailed its arms around, as though it thought it could shake the fire off, but the flames just rose even higher, before jumping to those mummies who were nearest. They went up in a moment, and more flames leaped to more dead bodies, racing up and down the street until the whole area was illuminated by burning figures.

I was worried the flames might jump to the buildings and set them alight, too, but it seemed the magical fires only had an appetite for mummies. One by one, burning shapes crashed to the ground, thrashing weakly as the fires ate them up. Mummies at the edge of the crowd turned to run, but the flames were quicker. Up and down the street, the mummies burned until finally there was nothing left but unmoving blackened bodies and guttering flames.

The Damned realized that Polly was still buried under a heap of charred shapes. He rushed over to her and tore the bodies away with his armoured hands. At the bottom of the pile, he found Polly lying curled up in a ball, smoke rising from her scorched fur. The Damned armoured down and beat out the last few flames with his bare hands, rather than risk hurting her with his armoured strength. Polly suddenly uncurled and jumped to her feet, bits of burnt hide falling away to reveal fresh new fur. She grinned broadly at Lex as he stood there, stunned.

'Werewolves heal, remember? It's what we do.'

Lex took her in his arms and hugged her tightly. Polly was too startled to hug him back, and Lex quickly let the werewolf go. Polly turned into her human form and stared at him.

'What was that for?'

'I was worried,' said Lex.

'Why?'

'Because I talked you into coming with me.'

'You couldn't have kept me away,' said Polly. 'I always dreamed of fighting alongside the Damned.'

'Yes,' said Lex. 'Another reason to feel guilty.'

'Don't,' Polly said briskly. 'I don't do guilt, and neither should you.'

'What else should the damned feel?' said Lex. 'It hurt me to see you hurt.'

'That's sweet,' said Polly. 'But really, you're far too old for me.'

'Well,' said Lex, 'that goes without saying.'

Polly looked around as Grace and I moved over to join the two of them.

'I'm fine!' she said loudly. 'Don't you start fussing.'

'Wouldn't dream of it,' I said. 'Just wanted to check you and the big guy were ready to move on. We still have a treasure house to find.'

'And loot,' said Grace.

'I hadn't forgotten,' I said.

And then we all looked around sharply as someone started applauding. A man and a woman were standing at the entrance to a side street. The man was clapping loudly, and the woman was smiling. It didn't seem to me to be a particularly pleasant smile. They walked unhurriedly over to join us, and my crew quickly moved to stand closer together. I glanced at Lex.

'Why haven't you put your armour back on?'

'I want them to see my face,' said Lex.

'That would certainly scare the hell out of me,' said Grace.

'Thank you,' said Lex.

I looked at Polly. 'Can I just tactfully remind you that you are no longer a wolf and are actually standing around in your skin?'

'Thought it was a bit draughty,' said Polly.

She became a werewolf again and took up her most threatening stance.

The new arrivals came to a halt a discreet distance away, and the man stopped applauding.

'Welcome to the undercity,' said the woman. 'I have to say, we're amazed to see you here, and not a little impressed. Hardly anyone gets this far. But then most people aren't the legendary Gideon Sable and his crew.'

Lex looked at me. 'You're legendary, but I'm just part of the crew?'

'They don't know you like I do,' I said.

Lex turned his cold stare back to the newcomers. 'That is about to change.'

'I am Cleopatra Bones,' said the woman. 'This is my husband, a Mime Called Malice. Call him Mal.'

Cleopatra was tall and voluptuous, a mature woman with sharp gypsy features and dark curly hair. She wore a sky-blue catsuit with two large guns holstered on her hips and bandoliers of bullets crossing her considerable chest. She smiled easily, but her hands never moved far from her guns. Her husband stood calmly at her side, ready for anything. A good head shorter than his wife, he had the painted white face, striped shirt and dark trousers of the traditional mime, but his smile had no humour in it, and his eyes were cold.

Lex took a step forward, and both the man and the woman gave him their full attention. If his scowling face frightened them, they were doing a really good job of hiding it.

'Where is Sally?' said Lex.

I don't think his voice had ever been colder, but Cleopatra just nodded easily.

'Keeping my father company. She's quite safe; he's become rather fond of her.' She gestured at the side street she and her husband had appeared from. 'The centre is just around the corner. Which is why you ran into all those mummies. Thanks for getting rid of them for us. They seemed like a good idea at the time, but the numbers have risen over the years, and they did clutter up the place terribly.'

'They were your idea?' I said.

'It was my idea to make use of them,' said Cleopatra. 'Now, since you're Gideon Sable, this must be Annie Anybody.'

'Call me Grace.'

'No,' said Cleopatra. 'And that leaves the little wolf girl

and the Damned. We know all about the Damned, because Little Miss Sticky Fingers won't shut up about him.'

'You're talking about my wife,' said Lex.

'We know!' said Cleopatra. 'If she tries to show us the wedding photos on her phone one more time . . .'

'Did I hear you right?' I said. 'Coldheart is your father?'

She nodded calmly. 'My husband and I run security for him, because he's so taken up with his current obsession that he tends to forget about practical things. And please, don't call him by that name. Coldheart is just a label that got slapped on him by his new business partner. My father is Leland Stevens.'

'Wait a minute,' I said. 'I know him! A minor collector, who used to hang around on the edges of the scene, picking up things no one else wanted and then finding specialized buyers who would pay through the nose for them. When did he become obsessed with hearing the sirens' song?'

Cleopatra stirred unhappily. 'Just recently. He's an old man now, and his mind isn't what it used to be. He is determined to become the first man in millennia to hear the song the sirens sang, no matter what it costs him.'

I looked at her thoughtfully. 'By any chance . . . would Leland's new business partner be Murray the Mentalist?'

'Of course you'd know him,' said Cleopatra. 'He's a thief and a cheat, just like you. My father needed someone to help him acquire state-of-the art sound technology, and since he won't ever leave this place, he had to take on a business partner to help with the heavy lifting. Murray came with excellent recommendations, which I'm pretty sure now he wrote himself, but at the time he seemed exactly what my father needed.'

Grace tugged surreptitiously at my arm. 'Why did Murray change the man's name to Coldheart?'

'Because it's all part of his con,' I said. 'Coldheart was never real. Just a name and a reputation, a scarecrow designed to appear bigger and more menacing than Leland Stevens ever could. Murray needed a threat I would feel obliged to deal with. No wonder I'd never heard of Coldheart or his marvellous treasures.' I nodded to Cleopatra. 'So this is where Leland ended up. I did wonder what happened to him.'

'You know my father?' said Cleopatra.

'Only by reputation,' I said. 'I have to say, I was expecting all manner of traps and guards, not just a bunch of walking corpses with serious moisture issues.'

'My father used up all of his money buying the sound tech,' said Cleopatra. 'A lifetime's savings, gone in less than a year. He even had to sell off most of his collection. After that, we didn't have enough left to pay the guards, so we had to let them go. There never were any traps; we didn't think we needed them after we moved this part of the undercity into our own pocket dimension.'

I fixed Cleopatra with my harshest stare. 'On the way here, we met an old man who said he was sent here by Judi Rifkin . . . but she's only been working on her own for a few years. So how could Michael Sharpe have aged so much in such a short time?'

'A side effect from the dimensional machine that put us outside everything,' said Cleopatra. 'How do you think we acquired so many mummies in such a short period?'

'You let them age to death,' I said. 'And then put them to work.'

'It's what they deserved,' said Cleopatra. 'For trying to steal from us.'

'Why didn't the machine age us?' said Grace.

'You had the Damned with you,' said Cleopatra. 'Just the proximity of his armour was enough to protect you.'

I nodded to Lex. 'I always knew you'd come in handy for something.'

Lex hadn't turned his cold stare away from Cleopatra. 'I'm here to take Sally home.'

'Well, you can't have her,' said Cleopatra. 'My father still needs her, so you'll just have to be patient. You can have her back when my father's finished with her. And not before.'

'I'm the Damned,' said Lex. 'I don't do patient.'

He put on his armour, and once again Heaven and Hell made themselves manifest in the world. Cleopatra fell back in spite of herself. Her husband Mal mimed a large club, surged forward and brought the invisible weapon crashing down on the Damned. The impact bludgeoned him down on to one knee before he could even raise an arm to defend himself. Polly threw herself at Mal and slammed him to the ground, her bared teeth straining for his throat.

They rolled back and forth, while Mal mimed a knife and thrust it into Polly's ribs again and again. But the wounds healed as fast as he could make them. Mal might be able to mime a knife, but apparently silver was beyond him. Polly's jaws inched closer to Mal's face.

The Damned was already back on his feet again. Cleopatra drew one of her guns and the Damned stopped where he was.

'That's right,' said Cleopatra. 'You recognize this gun, don't you? Call off your pet, Lex. Do it now!'

'Let the man go, Polly!' said the Damned.

The werewolf reluctantly disengaged and trotted back to crouch beside the Damned. The mime rose quickly to his feet and moved over to stand beside Cleopatra, who was still covering the Damned with her gun.

'Why did you call me off, Lex?' said Polly. 'I was having fun.'

'It's the gun,' I said.

Polly looked at the weapon in Cleopatra's hand. 'What's so special about that?'

'I've never seen it before,' I said. 'But I've read a lot about it. That is the Iscariot Device. The gun Lex used to murder two angels. Its bullets are made from the thirty pieces of silver paid to Judas to betray the Christ.'

'How many times can one weapon screw up my life?' said the Damned.

'My father acquired it from Old Harry's Place,' said Cleopatra. 'A birthday present for me, back when he still remembered such things. For the girl who has one of every other kind of weapon . . . These bullets will quite definitely punch through angelic armour, Lex, so behave yourself.'

'No,' said the Damned. 'I can't do that. I have to rescue Sally.'

'True love,' said Cleopatra, nodding approvingly. 'Somewhat rarer than it should be, these days. I salute you. But I can't let you do anything that might hurt my father.'

She raised the Iscariot Device and shot the Damned in the face.

I already had my hand inside my jacket pocket, holding the time pen, and I hit the button the moment Cleopatra raised her gun. All sound cut off as everything crashed to a halt. The world became suffused in a crimson glow as light sank down into the infra-red, and the air was suddenly thick as treacle.

I was only just in time; I could see the bullet hanging in mid-air, well on its way to the Damned's armoured face. It didn't look like any normal bullet. It seemed somehow more real than its surroundings, more *there* than anything else, and it gleamed silver even in the crimson half-light. It was still straining forward, fighting the inertia of stopped Time in its eagerness to get to its target.

I reached out and carefully closed my fist around the bullet, but even though I tugged at it with all my strength, I couldn't deflect the bullet from its intended target. I couldn't even stop it edging stubbornly forward. I let go and moved over to the Damned. I put my arms around him, intending to carry him away from the line of fire. But the Damned in his armour was far too heavy to move.

I let go of him and thought quickly. I was already starting to run out of breath. I put my shoulder against the Damned and slowly forced him to one side. It took all of my strength, but I kept him moving until he was no longer in front of the bullet. By then I was exhausted, and my lungs were screaming for air. I looked back at the bullet to make sure the Damned was safe and then hit the button on the pen again.

Time took over, and the silver bullet screamed past the Damned's face. Before Cleopatra could fire the gun again, the Damned lunged forward and slapped the Iscariot Device out of her hand. It hit the ground, and Polly kicked it out of reach. Grace moved quickly over to hold me up, as I struggled to get some air back into my lungs.

'What the hell just happened?' said Polly, looking quickly from where I had been to where I was now.

I managed a smile for her. 'I stole a march on Time.'

'Always a thief,' said Cleopatra. 'I should have known.'

Mal stepped forward, putting himself between the Damned and his wife. The Damned started toward him, but I raised a staying hand.

'I think we need to calm things down a little, Lex.'

'Give me one good reason why I shouldn't kill them,' he said.

'Because we're thieves, not killers.'

'That's you, not me. What's two more deaths to the Damned?'

'We don't know enough about the situation we're in,' I said carefully. 'I get the feeling these two might be just as much victims of Murray's con as we are. I'm asking you to give me some time, to get more answers.'

'You ask a lot, Gideon.'

'Because I'm worth it,' I said. 'And so are you.' I turned to Cleopatra. 'Tell me the truth, if you want to live. Where's the minotaur?'

She looked at me blankly. 'What minotaur? Our only guards were the mummies.'

'Of course,' I said. 'Murray does love to play his little games.'

'I don't understand,' said Grace. 'What does Murray have to do with what's happening here?'

'Murray has been behind everything, right from the beginning,' I said. 'We've been dancing to his tune all along.'

'Did I just hear my name being taken in vain?' said Murray.

We all turned to look, and there he was, leaning carelessly against his standing mirror. Still dressed like an old-time magician, though he was no longer bothering with the black turban. He smiled easily back at us and rubbed his hands together briskly.

'Well, things seem to have sorted themselves out pretty much as I anticipated. That's what good planning and underhanded forethought will do for you.' He nodded to me. 'Have you worked it out yet?'

'I think so,' I said. 'I've known for some time that you had to be far more involved in all of this than you seemed. You knew too much, and all along this whole thing has felt a lot like *Let's you and him fight.* You sent us here because you needed someone who could take down Cleopatra and Malice; because, for all your skills, you were never a fighter. You set this whole thing up, from Sally's kidnapping to stealing our

stone, just so you could manoeuvre us into the proper frame
of mind to do your dirty work for you.'

'You always were the clever one, Gideon,' said Murray.

'I knew you had to be running some kind of con,' I said.
'Because that's what you do. But you confirmed my suspicions
with all that nonsense about being inside a city's dream. Cities
don't dream; only the living do that. It was just one of your
illusions, designed to throw us off balance. So was the massive
shadow we saw, in the city and on the Low Road – put there
to pile on the pressure and keep us moving, so we wouldn't
have time to think about what was happening. I realized the
shadow was just an illusion when I noticed that none of
the dead could see it. You're good, Murray, but not good
enough to fool the dead.'

'Ah, Gideon,' said Murray, shaking his head sadly. 'And
you were doing so well . . .'

'What have I missed?' I said.

'Why I ran this con in the first place,' said Murray.
'Everything that's happened to you so far is my revenge for
killing Honest John.'

Grace and I looked at each other. That wasn't a name we'd
expected to hear again.

'What's he got to do with this?' said Grace.

'Honest John? A businessman with no surname, only a
reputation? I'm amazed you didn't guess long ago. Honest
John was just another of my personas. His warehouse business
funded all my other lives, made it possible for us to stay hidden
and safe. When you killed him, you took all of that away.'

'But he made a mint from that warehouse!' said Grace. 'If
there was that much money to go round, why did you and
Osiris need to play con games?'

'Because it was fun,' said Murray. 'And because people
would have asked questions if we hadn't.'

'Honest John cheated us,' said Grace. 'He nearly destroyed us!'

Murray shrugged. 'It was just business.'

'He ordered his people to kill us,' I said.

'He knew you had the time pen,' said Murray. 'He expected
you to use it to escape. He didn't need to die.'

'All of this has been one big confidence trick,' I said.

'Persuading us to us look in one direction, while the real deal was going on somewhere else.'

Murray smiled happily. 'Right from the beginning. When Honest John was murdered, I appeared to take his place, because I'm the default persona. And after a little thought, I set all of this in motion. I've been giving everyone a little push, from the shadows. I even put the idea of contacting Madam Osiris into your head, Gideon. It was all down to me, keeping the game moving, forever one step ahead . . .'

'I thought you were my friend,' I said.

'You put an end to that when you killed one of me,' said Murray. 'I'd already decided I needed someone to get rid of Cleo and Mal, and you and your crew made the perfect patsies. It's a poor con that can't multitask. Everyone here has been dancing to my tune all along. My siren song – to lure you in and destroy you.'

Polly glared at Murray. 'You were using us? No one uses me!'

She started forward, only to stop abruptly as Murray raised his hand and showed us he was holding the Iscariot Device. I wondered how I could have lost track of such an important thing, but that was Murray's gift: to keep your attention fixed where he wanted it, and away from what was really going on.

'I always was a picker-up of unconsidered trifles,' he said happily, aiming the gun at Polly. 'Silver bullets, remember?'

'Why did you insist that Polly be a part of this, Murray?' I said quickly, to bring his attention back to me.

Murray kept his gaze fixed on Polly. 'You don't remember me, do you, little wolf girl? I came to you for help, on a con that could have benefitted us both greatly . . . but you just blew me off. So making you a part of this is my little revenge.'

'I'll get you for this,' said Polly.

'I don't think so,' said Murray.

He shot her. The bullet's impact sent her crashing to the ground, blood pouring from her side. The Damned armoured down so he could hold her in his arms, and she clung to him like a child. She tried to say something, but blood sprayed past her teeth, choking her words.

'Always be prepared, Gideon,' said Murray. 'And do unto others before they get a chance to do it to you. One of the first things I taught you.'

'You bastard,' said Lex. 'You didn't have to do that.'

'I think I did,' said Murray. 'Put your hand over the wound, Lex. Stop the bleeding.'

Lex pressed his hand hard over the wound in Polly's side. She groaned loudly, but the bleeding slowed.

'That's right, Lex,' said Murray. 'As long as you stay there and do that, you're keeping her alive. And not bothering me.'

'Bastard!' said Lex.

'You already said that,' said Murray.

Polly pressed her hand over Lex's. 'If I die, kill him.'

'Love to,' said Lex.

'When did you become so cold-blooded, Murray?' I said.

'I always was. You just didn't want to see it.'

'Talk to me, Murray,' I said. 'How is this revenge of your supposed to work?'

I wanted him focused on me, to give one of the others a chance to edge out of the line of fire and jump him. I took a step forward, but instead of covering me with the Iscariot Device, Murray pointed the gun at Grace.

'You might be angry enough to risk your own life,' Murray said smugly. 'But not Annie Anybody's. Now, tell me what you've worked out so far. Show me what a good pupil you are.'

'This is all about Coldheart,' I said. 'Or, to be more exact, Leland Stevens.'

'I gave him the new name,' said Murray. 'Told him it was all about branding, and he believed me! The man is in his dotage. Should have retired long ago.'

'Ostensibly, you became his partner so you could supply him with the technology he needed,' I said. 'But really it was all about gaining access to this place. So you could steal his identity and replace him.'

'Got it in one,' said Murray. 'That was my original con, before I decided I needed to take you down as well.'

'What are you talking about?' said Cleopatra.

'Slow, isn't she?' said Murray.

'I think we've all been a bit slow,' I said. 'But I'm catching up. This has simply been about Murray needing to become someone new.'

'And make a lot of money along the way,' said Murray.

'You made yourself rich by making my father poor!' said Cleopatra.

'That's how business works, dear,' said Murray. 'Now, hush. Adults are talking.' He nodded to me. 'You gave me the original idea. When I learned you'd reinvented yourself as the new Gideon Sable, that gave me the idea to become the new Coldheart. So, really, you could say everything that's happened is your fault.'

'Why would you want to be my father?' said Cleopatra. One of her hands was inching closer to her remaining gun, but she knew she couldn't try anything as long as Murray had the Iscariot Device. A weapon like that could kill us all in a moment.

Murray looked to me, to answer Cleopatra's question.

'Because your father's a hermit,' I said. 'No one would notice when someone else took over his life.'

'You are doing well!' said Murray. 'Now, now, don't frown at me like that, Gideon. I was forced into this.'

'What happened?' I said. 'Did your past finally start catching up with you?'

'Time has not been kind to me,' said Murray. 'I have been pursued for so long, by so many enemies . . . Forced to live small and inconsequential lives when I could have been so much more. I needed a way out. So I created the legend of the mysterious hermit Coldheart, and his incredibly dangerous security chiefs, and then I set up the kidnapping of Sally, to establish Coldheart as the villain of the piece. Of course, once he had her, she was perfect to get the rock back from you and bring you into the game. I knew if I made Coldheart seem big and bad and powerful enough, you wouldn't be able to resist going after him. Particularly if you thought you were charging to the rescue of a damsel in distress. All I had to do then was point you at Cleopatra and Malice, and let you take care of them for me.'

'So there'd be nobody left to protect Leland,' I said. 'When you came to kill him.'

'Of course,' said Murray. 'The world isn't big enough for two Coldhearts. I've never been a man of violence myself, not when there's some gullible soul I can con into doing such things for me. I left the insulting note in Sally's hotel room after she was kidnapped, to make sure Lex would be angry enough to start killing again. In fact, I really thought Cleopatra and Malice would be dead by the time I got here . . .'

'None of us were supposed to survive this, were we?' I said. 'We all have to die, to make sure no one can tell the world about your becoming Coldheart.'

'Plans always work best when there's no one left to explain how the trick was done,' said Murray. 'I did tell you there was a monster in the story, Gideon. And you're looking at him.'

I glared at Murray, and he met my gaze steadily. His smile never wavered.

'I thought we were friends,' I said.

'Oh, grow up, Gideon,' said Murray. 'There's no room for sentiment in the world of the con. This will be my greatest triumph – and my last. Murray and Osiris and all the others will simply vanish, gone without a trace, as I become the solitary hermit Coldheart. My enemies will stop looking, and I will be safe and secure at last.'

'I'll see you dead before I let you touch my father,' said Cleopatra, her voice flat and cold.

Murray just smiled at her. 'Not while I've got the Iscariot Device.'

'You can't hold all of us off indefinitely,' I said.

'Never thought I could,' said Murray. 'This is just to keep you in line, until the real executioner arrives.'

'What are you talking about?' said Grace. 'Who else is there?'

Murray smiled smugly. 'Remember the shadow that pursued you? There's a reason why it looked so convincing and felt so threatening. That is my sleeping partner in this little game I've organized. It hid my powers when I created the illusion of the city's dream, so none of my enemies would notice. The whole point of putting you in that place was to make it possible for the Great Shadow to get your scent. It's on its way here, right now, so I can sacrifice all of you to it.'

'How is it going to get in?' said Cleopatra. 'This whole area is shielded and protected.'

'But when your father invited me in to discuss business matters, I was able to quietly establish my very own back door,' said Murray.

'Of course,' I said. 'You have the travelling mirror. But how is a shadow that big going to get through Albert?'

'It doesn't need to,' said Murray. 'The Great Shadow is a power and a force beyond reckoning. It swims through dimensions like a shark on the prowl. It can go anywhere, and it does. I should know; the Great Shadow is one of the demons that have been pursuing me all these years. But I did a little research and discovered that there were other things this particular demon wanted more than me. So I got in touch and made a deal. I've always been very good at that. The Great Shadow has agreed to forgive and forget all my crimes against it, in return for all of you. A very tasty mix of assorted legends. The Damned, Gideon Sable, Annie Anybody, Switch It Sally, Polly Perkins – and Cleopatra Bones and Malice for dessert.'

'What is this Great Shadow?' I said. 'I've never even heard of it.'

Murray shrugged. 'It's heard of you. And especially the Damned. It really wants those halos. I think, in its own way, the Great Shadow is a bit of a collector.'

I took another step forward, and Murray raised the Iscariot Device threateningly, still targeting Grace. I was careful not to look at her, glaring coldly at Murray instead. I wanted him thinking about me, not her.

'You might not be my friend any more, Murray,' I said, 'but I'm not just talking to you. Wherever you go, your other selves go with you. Madam Osiris and I have been through a lot together, and I think we're still friends.'

'She has been forced into the background,' said Murray. 'I'm the one in the driving seat.'

'I'm betting she can still hear me,' I said. 'Osiris, I need your help!'

Murray frowned. 'Stop that, Gideon. You're embarrassing yourself.'

'Osiris!' I said. 'You have as much right to exist here as he does! Help me stop him, before he kills you off, along with us.'

Murray looked suddenly confused, as though troubled by an intrusive thought. His face twisted, the features becoming suddenly vague and indistinct. His hands began to tremble, and the gun slowly lowered. Murray the Mentalist fell back a step, and somebody else stepped forward.

Madam Osiris was a middle-aged woman, dressed like a gypsy seer from some old Hollywood movie. Wrapped in traditional robes, topped with a white silk turban, she had a handsome face under industrial-strength levels of makeup, dominated by two glowing crystal balls where her eyes should have been. Cheap plastic bangles rattled noisily on her muscular arms as she stretched slowly, relaxing into her new form.

'No need to shout, Gideon; I was never far away.'

'And I thought *my* life was complicated,' said Grace.

'I don't understand,' said Cleopatra. 'Who is this?'

'Murray is just one of many personalities who share a single existence,' I said. 'There used to be just him, and then he added a whole bunch of other identities to help him work his cons. But after he made the mistake of upsetting a particularly vindictive spirit, they became just as real as him.'

'Never mess with a pookah,' said Osiris. 'They have a really mean sense of humour.'

'Good to see you again, Osiris,' I said. 'I thought we were in trouble there for a minute. But then you always did have a knack for appearing in the nick of time.'

'What are old friends for?' said Madam Osiris. 'Sorry about Murray. You know what he's like.'

'I thought I did,' I said.

And then Osiris looked down at the gun in her hand.

'I don't remember this . . .'

She frowned, as though troubled by some unpleasant thought, and the moment's distraction was all it took. In a moment, Osiris was gone, and Murray was back. He quickly aimed the Iscariot Device at Grace again, his hand entirely steady.

'That is quite enough of that,' he said sharply. 'You never were as strong as me, Osiris. You never had the ambition. Once the Great Shadow gets here, I'll feed you to it, along with all my other selves. And then I'll be free of all of you, at last. Free to be just me.'

'Osiris!' I said. 'Fight him!'

'You're wasting your time, Gideon,' said Murray. 'She caught me by surprise once, but that won't happen again. I will always be the most important of my selves, because I was here first.'

And then he looked over my shoulder, and something in his smile made all of us turn to follow his gaze. A deep, dark shadow was advancing down the street towards us, swallowing up the street lamps one by one. I could feel the cold and awful weight of it, pressing down on the world. It wasn't just darkness; it was the complete absence of light and hope. I finally understood why the dead on the Low Road hadn't been able to see it: the Great Shadow only preyed on the living.

I turned back to Murray, and he smiled easily.

'And so we come at last to the end of the con, Gideon. But first, I want you to reach inside your jacket, slowly and carefully, and take out your time pen. Don't get any ideas . . . Albert has some power over Time, as well as Space. He can slow its passing down enough that even if you do activate your pen, I'll still be able to shoot Grace. And you don't want that, do you, Gideon?'

'No,' I said.

'I did try to teach you that friends are nothing but a burden,' said Murray. 'But you never listened. Take out the pen.'

I did so, slowly and carefully, and held it out before me.

'Good boy,' said Murray. 'Now drop it on the ground and kick it over to me. And say goodbye to your last chance of stopping me.'

I dropped the pen. And while everyone was busy watching it fall, I played my trump card.

'Sandra! I need you!'

There was a blast of trumpets and a roar of Hosannahs, as

Sandra Ransom walked out of the standing mirror and smiled happily around her.

'I thought you'd forgotten all about me, Gideon.'

'I remembered you saying that if I ever really needed you, I should feel free to call on you at any time,' I said. 'You made such a point of it that I knew it had to be important, so I always kept the thought of you in reserve. But I had to wait for just the right moment.'

'Well, here I am, to save the day.'

Murray stared at her, frozen in place with shock and horror. 'You can't be here!'

'I think you'll find I can,' said Sandra. 'No doors are closed to me.' She looked down the street at the advancing Great Shadow and raised her voice. 'Go home! Don't make me have to come over there!'

The shadow stopped and then slowly faded away. Because it knew its mistress's voice when it heard it. One by one, the street lights returned, and the darkness disappeared. Murray's face twisted like a thwarted child, and he turned abruptly to aim the Iscariot Device at Sandra. She looked at it thoughtfully and started to say something, but Lex cut across her.

'Please, Polly is dying. You must help her.'

'Not right now,' said Sandra, her gaze fixed on Murray. 'I'm busy.'

'Please,' I said.

'Oh, all right!' Sandra gestured abruptly, and Polly froze where she was. Blood no longer flowed from the wound in her side. Lex was completely still as well, and I understood immediately what had happened. I'd stopped Time often enough to know it when I saw it.

'Thank you, Sandra,' I said.

'I hate distractions,' said Sandra. 'Now, where was I? Oh, yes!'

She smiled at Murray, and he stood very still. All the colour had drained out of his face.

'No wonder I couldn't see where Sally was being held,' said Sandra. 'You used the Great Shadow's power to hide her from me.'

'I still have powers of my own,' said Murray.

'Go ahead,' said Sandra. 'Try them. See how far that gets you.'

'Even you can't stand up to the Iscariot Device!' Murray said loudly. 'This gun was made to kill angels!'

'Angels,' said Sandra, dismissively.

The Iscariot Device jumped out of Murray's grasp and shot across the intervening space to nestle into Sandra's waiting hand.

'Nasty little thing,' she said.

She opened her hand, and the Iscariot Device was gone. The whole atmosphere in the street seemed to ease, as though a rabid killer had just been escorted away by men in white coats.

'Did you just destroy it?' I said. 'I didn't think that was possible.'

'I sent it away,' said Sandra. 'Somewhere safe. Because it's always possible that there will come a day when humanity might need a weapon that can destroy angels.'

'Have you been watching us the whole time?' said Grace.

'I've been keeping an eye on things ever since Gideon first called me,' said Sandra. 'I could tell something was going on.'

'I was hoping I wouldn't need you,' I said. 'I owe you enough already.'

'Don't think I've forgotten,' said Sandra. She looked coldly at Murray, and he shuddered under the weight of her gaze. Sandra smiled, and not in a good way. 'You have been a very bad boy, Murray. I mean, you always were, when you weren't being a bad girl, but this time you've crossed the line. I think it's time to put you back in the box.'

'What are you going to do?' said Murray, glaring back at her defiantly. 'Lock me up in a cell? I'll escape. I always do. Punish me? I'll get my own back, and you know it. I'll make everyone here pay!'

'No, you won't. I've arranged a nice little get-together for you,' said Sandra. 'All your old enemies are waiting to meet you. They got really excited when I told them I'd found you. They've been looking forward to this for such a long time. Oh, the plans they have for you!'

'Wait!' I said.

Sandra turned her perfect head to look at me. 'Wait?'

'I didn't call you here just to kill him,' I said.

'Oh, he isn't going to die,' said Sandra. 'What the demons have in mind will be much worse than that. And can you honestly say he doesn't deserve it? He was quite ready to watch you die.'

'That's Murray,' I said. 'Not all his personas are like that. I can't speak for the others, but Osiris was always kind to me. She doesn't deserve to be punished along with him.'

'Oh, all right!' Sandra snapped. 'You do love to complicate things, don't you!'

And just like that, there were two figures standing before her: Murray the Mentalist and Madam Osiris. It would have been hard to say which of them looked most surprised.

'Separated at last,' said Madam Osiris. 'You have no idea how good it feels, not to have his thoughts lurking around in the back of my head. Thank you, Gideon.' And then she looked at Sandra Ransom. 'I know the rules. What is this going to cost me?'

'I'll have to think about it,' said Sandra.

'Put it on my bill,' I said.

Sandra smiled at me radiantly. 'You do like to live dangerously, don't you, Gideon? Very well . . . Get out of here, Osiris, and don't bother me again.'

Madam Osiris nodded quickly and walked over to the standing mirror. 'Hello, Albert. Good to see you again. Home, please, and don't spare the horses.'

'Of course, Madam,' said Albert.

Osiris stepped through the mirror in a last jangle of plastic bangles and was gone. Sandra turned back to Murray. He looked at me desperately.

'You gave me your word you'd protect me!'

'That was from the Damned,' I said.

'I was your friend!'

'Were you?'

Sandra laughed, and Murray turned back to face her.

'It's time for you to go now,' she said. 'Who knows, after enough time doing penance, you might even emerge as a better person. Miracles do happen.'

'You should know,' I said.

Sandra laughed softly. 'Open wide, Albert.'

'My pleasure, Miss Ransom,' said the mirror.

An unseen force picked Murray up and threw him at the mirror. He screamed as he saw what was waiting for him on the other side, and then he passed through, and his scream was cut off. I turned my head away. Grace came over and took me in her arms.

'He would have killed us all, Gideon.'

'I was still his friend,' I said. 'Even if he wasn't mine.'

I let go of Grace, and she let go of me. Sandra was talking quietly to Albert, so I stooped down and quietly gathered up the time pen from the floor. You never know when you might need some backup, talking to God's little sister. She turned suddenly and smiled at me.

'Thanks to you, I was able to put right an old wrong. And a whole bunch of very powerful entities now owe me, big time. So we're even. You don't owe me anything.'

'That's good to know,' I said.

She raised an eyebrow at the coldness in my voice. 'I got rid of Murray, so you wouldn't have to. What are friends for?'

'If you want to show your gratitude,' I said, 'help Polly.'

Sandra looked at the frozen wolf girl dying in the frozen man's arms, and then back at me. 'If I do, you'll owe me again.'

'I can live with that,' I said.

Sandra thought about it and then shook her head. 'Sorry. I'm busy.'

Sandra Ransom walked back into the standing mirror, and Polly and Lex dropped back into Time. Polly shrank back into her human form and lay exhausted in Lex's arms. Her eyes were closed, and her breathing was so shallow I couldn't see her breast move. Blood pulsed sluggishly past the hand Lex still had pressed against the wound in her side. He looked at me helplessly.

'There's nothing I can do for her. I only know how to destroy lives, not save them. Isn't there anything you can do?'

'I'm thinking,' I said.

Lex looked down at Polly, his face full of unfamiliar

emotions. 'I brought her into this, and look what happened to her. All I ever do is hurt the people I care for. There's a reason they call me the Damned.'

'I have an idea,' I said, turning to face Cleopatra. 'There's no reason why we should be enemies. We were all victims of Murray's plans, so let's call a truce. Go get Switch It Sally and bring her here.'

Cleopatra looked at Mal, and he nodded quickly. Cleopatra hurried off around the corner. I looked steadily at Lex.

'Everything's going to be all right. Just keep your hand pressed on that wound, and Polly will be fine. Trust me.'

'That's not easy, Gideon,' said Lex.

'But you're worth it,' I said. 'Both of you.'

Mal cleared his throat, and when he started speaking in a deep and sonorous voice, I think we all jumped just a little.

'You're welcome to Sally,' he said. 'She's been driving us crazy. We only hung on to her because she's been such good company for Leland. She keeps him happy and grounded, which is unfortunately more than his daughter can manage.' He looked directly at Lex. 'Your wife has been treated well.'

'You're still holding her prisoner,' said Lex.

'I'm pretty sure Cleo will let her go now,' said Malice. 'Rather than fight a war we don't have to. She doesn't want to believe how far gone her father is, but without Sally around to prop him up, I think she'll finally have to. It's time Leland was put somewhere he can be properly looked after.'

'What about the stone?' I said.

'We never wanted Leland to have it,' said Malice. 'It just played into his obsession over the sirens' song, so that he couldn't think about anything else. Not even his own daughter. So we decided to take the stone and give it to you.'

'I thought I recognized that voice!' I said. 'You're the one who brought the stone to our shop!'

'Yes,' said Malice. 'Cleo and I thought the stone would be safe in your hands. But Murray found out you had it and talked Leland into using Sally to get it back. He wanted Leland distracted, and now we know why.'

Cleopatra came hurrying back round the corner, with Sally beside her. Dressed in a blindingly white pants suit, Sally was as dark-skinned, blonde-haired and elegant as ever. She squealed loudly as she saw Lex, and ran towards him. He gently lowered Polly to the ground and stood up, and Sally threw herself into his arms. They held each other tightly, and then Lex pushed Sally away. She looked a little hurt, but before she could say anything, Lex gestured at Polly, lying bloody and broken on the ground.

'What's this, darling?' said Sally, arching an elegant eyebrow. 'Polly Perkins? What is she doing here?'

'She's part of the crew now,' said Lex. 'Her tracking skills helped us find you.'

'She's been shot with a silver bullet,' I said. 'We need your gift, to save her.'

Sally gave Lex a hard look. 'You seem very concerned over the little tramp, darling. I hope you haven't been straying in my absence.'

'She's been very brave,' said Lex. 'And, of course, I care for her. She's the daughter I always wanted and never had.'

Sally smiled suddenly. 'Of course. I quite understand. And I know exactly what to do! Stand back and make way for Nurse Sally!'

She waggled a closed fist at Polly, and when she opened her hand, a silver bullet was lying in her palm.

'I just switched out the silver bullet and replaced it with a lead one from Cleo's bandolier,' she said grandly. 'And what's lead to a werewolf?'

Polly was already scrabbling on to her feet. She put a hand to her side, but the wound was gone. She worked her mouth for a moment and then spat out a lead bullet. She laughed happily and then looked at Lex.

'I was dying, not deaf. I'm your daughter? Don't I get a say in the matter?'

'No,' said Lex.

She grinned. 'Suits me. You're everything I ever admired. I can have new cards made, saying *The Daughter of the Damned*. My asking price just went way up.' She broke off to look at Sally. 'Saved by Switch It Sally; I'll never live this down.'

'Get over yourself, darling,' said Sally. She smiled fondly

at Lex. 'When we get back to Paris, let's see what we can do about making you a real daughter.'

'I love a happy ending,' said Grace.

'First things first,' I said. 'The job isn't over yet. We didn't go through all of this just to leave empty-handed. I want my stone back.'

'Of course,' said Grace. 'It isn't the principle of the thing; it's the money.'

'My father still has it,' said Cleopatra. 'But you'll have to ask him where it is. If he remembers.'

'I remember,' said Sally. 'I did all of his remembering for him.'

I nodded to Lex and Polly. 'You two keep an eye on Cleopatra and Malice. Sally, Grace, you come with me. I want to talk to Leland.'

'Better let me do it, darling,' said Sally. 'He's not good with strangers. He's not good with family. That's the only reason they kept me around.' She stopped to look at Grace. 'Nice leathers, darling. They don't suit you.'

'If Lex is Polly's father now,' Grace said sweetly, 'Does that make you the evil stepmother?'

'Let's get going,' I said quickly.

EIGHT
Time For One Last Song.

We rounded the corner, and there at last was the treasure house we'd come so far to find. It was just a great big barn, with no frills or graces. The windows had been painted black, and the front door was standing open. I looked at Sally.

'This is the centre? It looks like a discount carpet warehouse.'

'Trust me, it looks even worse inside,' said Sally.

'What about Coldheart?' I said. 'Are you sure he's in there?'

'Of course, darling,' said Sally. 'I only just left him. He never leaves the centre. His psycho daughter sees to that.'

'I thought he wanted to be a hermit?' said Grace.

'Oh, he does,' said Sally. 'But sometimes he forgets that, and then his psycho daughter locks him in.'

'Why?' said Grace.

'You'll understand when you meet him,' said Sally.

'Take us to Coldheart,' I said. 'I want to retrieve our piece of stone, grab anything else worth having and then get the hell out of here.'

'Well, obviously, I'm all for that, darling,' said Sally.

The inside of the warehouse was mostly open space. Fluorescent tube lights provided a harsh and unforgiving illumination, but it wasn't as if there was much to see. Certainly nothing worth stealing. Pieces of unfamiliar technology stood around like the kind of aloof party guests no one would want to talk to. There was no sign of Coldheart anywhere.

I turned to Sally, but she got her answer in before I could even start the question.

'I know, I know: where's Coldheart? Honestly, darling,

you're like a two-year-old who wants his ice cream. Stick with me and I'll find him for you.'

She headed confidently off into the far reaches of the warehouse, her high heels clattering loudly on the bare concrete floor, as though to announce she was on her way. I went quickly after her, determined not to be left behind, and Grace moved along with me, maintaining a diplomatic silence. I kept a watchful eye on the various pieces of equipment we passed, standing alone like modern art on display. Most of them seemed to be working at something. Coloured lights blinked wisely, while dense streams of information flowed across the monitor screens. Every single machine seemed to be humming thoughtfully, as though quietly contemplating the mysteries of existence.

I couldn't shake the feeling that some of the machines were looking back at me, and not in a good way. As though we were walking through an electronic forest on the way to Grandma's cottage, knowing that the bad thing had already got there ahead of us. Coldheart was waiting, and while he might have started out as a legend created by Murray, there was always the chance that Leland might have grown into the role. I glanced at Grace.

'Do you recognize any of this stuff?'

'Not a thing,' said Grace. 'I'm guessing this is the state-of-the-art sonic technology that Leland spent all his money on, but I wouldn't know sonic if it fell on me. Was Murray an expert in that field?'

'It's possible,' I said. 'He'd been around long enough to have a persona who was good at everything. And I think Leland would have done enough research that he could spot a ringer or a lemon.'

'Do you really believe these machines can get the sirens' song out of the stone?'

'Wouldn't surprise me,' I said.

Grace looked at me sharply as she took in the tone of my voice.

'And we think this is not a good idea because . . .?'

'The sirens created their song specifically to lure men to their deaths,' I said. 'It's hardly going to be a toe-tapper, is it?'

'Oh, do keep up, darlings!'

Sally had come to a halt some distance ahead of us and was looking back impatiently. Grace and I took our time catching up with her, refusing to be hurried. Sally immediately started off again, throwing words back over her shoulder.

'You know, it's about time you turned up to rescue me, darlings. I have been going out of my mind, trapped in this godawful place while doing my best to keep the old man happy. And you needn't look at me like that; it was all about chatting cheerfully, making him cups of tea and doing my best to keep his psycho daughter off my back. She couldn't look after her own father, but she could always find time to tell me how to do it. And the food was awful. What took you so long?'

'It wasn't easy tracking you down,' I said. 'There were . . . complications, along the way.'

Sally sniffed loudly. 'It's your own fault for trusting Murray. I could have told you . . .'

'Where is Coldheart?' I said.

'Say that one more time,' Sally said ominously, 'and I will tell Lex what you and I used to get up to before I met him.'

I was careful to not even glance at Grace. 'I deny everything.'

'You think Lex will take your word over mine?'

'Of course,' I said. 'Because he knows you, and he knows me.'

'Well, honestly,' said Sally.

'You don't know the meaning of the word,' said Grace. 'You stole our rock!'

'Well, it wasn't my idea, darling!' said Sally. 'I could have switched out any number of far more interesting items, but all psycho daughter and her creepy better half wanted was the rock. So I settled for that.'

'Good of you,' said Grace.

Sally beamed. 'I thought so!'

'Where is Coldheart?' I said.

Sally sighed deeply. 'Wandering around somewhere. I can't keep track of him, because half the time even he doesn't know where he's going. He has a lot on his mind, and he can't listen to all of it at once. It's not as though I can call him to me, like a really big dog. I know – I've tried. Honestly, I feed him and encourage him and keep him from sticking his fingers into live sockets, and he still doesn't give a damn about anything except this stupid song he wants to hear.' She glowered about her. 'He keeps trying to explain what all this stuff is for, and I do wish he wouldn't. I don't speak Science.'

'I thought the old man was supposed to be senile?' said Grace.

'He's always seemed sharp enough to me,' said Sally. 'Just seriously absent-minded when it comes to anything that doesn't interest him. And I mean, well, away with the faeries, sometimes. It isn't enough that I have to remind him where the chemical toilet is; there are times when I worry I'll have to get it out and point it for him. I was supposed to be his companion, not his nanny!'

She stopped suddenly to peer suspiciously behind a towering piece of advanced science that looked as though it might be thinking about how best to land a Starbucks on the moon. She shook her head and glared off into the distance.

'Where has that man got to . . .? Let's try his private studio, where the main computers are. He always enjoys talking to them.'

She led us deeper into the warehouse. I glanced back at the front door, and it seemed a long way away. The hulking pieces of equipment looked like the standing stones of some high-tech henge; intent on solving some problem mere mortals could never hope to understand. Finally, we came to a halt before a large steel door that had been left slightly ajar. Set into a dividing wall that sealed off the whole end of the warehouse, the door looked thick enough to stop a bazooka at point-blank range. Sally grabbed hold of the door with both hands and started to pull it open, but after a moment I moved in to stop her so I could study the interior of the door. Sally shifted impatiently.

'What is there to look at, darling? It's just a door!'

'This looks to me like heavy-duty soundproofing,' I said. 'Why would Leland need something like that?'

'How would I know?' said Sally. 'But you wanted to meet Coldheart, so this is where we have to go.'

Grace moved in beside me. 'You think this is some kind of trap, Gideon?'

'There's more going on here than I can get my head around,' I said. 'I've seen doors that were designed to seal off bank vaults that looked less complicated than this. But . . . we didn't come all this way to turn back now.'

'Of course not,' said Grace. 'Perish the thought that we should do something sensible, just because we've run into something we don't understand.'

I smiled at her. 'Are you saying you don't want the possibly extremely valuable stone any more?'

She didn't smile back. 'When I walk into danger with you, it's because I can usually be sure you have some kind of plan to deal with it. But you don't know what's going on here, do you?'

'No,' I said. 'But I am sure of one thing. No one steals from us and gets away with it.'

In the end, it needed all three of us to push the door open enough that we could enter. I took a moment to get my breath back and then looked thoughtfully at Sally.

'How do you manage when we're not here?'

'It usually opens and shuts on its own, darling. I don't think it likes you.'

Coldheart's private studio turned out to be a complete mess. There were any number of computers, but most of the open space was taken up by a mattress on the floor, piles of discarded blankets and all kinds of discarded fast-food containers. The computers jammed up against each other, as though jostling for superiority, and the single workbench was littered with scientific papers. I took a quick look, but even if I had been able to read the cramped handwriting, I was pretty sure I wouldn't have been able to understand any of it. We had entered a mad scientist's den, where visitors were unexpected and unwelcome.

'You couldn't clean up this place with a flame-thrower,' said Grace.

'Trust me, darling, I know,' said Sally. 'Some men shouldn't be allowed to live on their own. You should see what Lex does with his socks.'

Grace pulled a face. 'What is that smell?'

'You really don't want to know,' Sally said darkly. 'Leland won't let me clean up in here in case I move something – and then how would he ever find it? I know squatters with personality disorders who live in less squalid conditions than this.'

'Yes,' I said, 'I'm sure you do.'

And then Grace and I both jumped a little as the door slammed shut behind us and locked itself.

'Don't worry,' Sally said quickly. 'It does that.'

I moved quickly back to look for a handle or some kind of release, but there didn't seem to be one.

'Don't try to force it!' Sally said quickly. 'The door is programmed to seal off the studio when the computers tell it to.'

'Why would they need to do that?' I asked.

'What he said, only louder,' said Grace.

Sally shrugged. 'To protect the equipment and make sure the old man stays put once he's in here. Psycho daughter's idea.'

'What happens when Coldheart wants to leave?' said Grace.

'Please don't call him that to his face,' said Sally, glancing quickly around. 'He really doesn't like it.'

'What do you call him?' I said.

'Darling, mostly,' said Sally. 'You know I'm no good with names.'

'I think I'll stick with Leland,' I said. 'So how does he get out of here, when he needs to?'

'He has to wait,' said Sally. 'Psycho daughter can override the door from outside, but mostly she doesn't. She likes knowing where her father is. I think she's a bit frightened of him, to be honest. Or of his work. All I know is, I've had to spend hours locked in this hellhole with the old man, nodding encouragingly while he talks to his computers instead of me.'

'And you never found a way out?' I said.

'Well, obviously I tried, darling. I can usually persuade most locks to see things my way, but that door is something else.'

'Why did you agree to be the old man's companion?' said Grace.

Sally scowled at her. 'You think I had a choice? I was kidnapped! They promised they'd let me go once I got them the rock, but first they had to bring it back here so the old man could authenticate it, and then they noticed how much he warmed to me . . . And suddenly I had to be his *companion*. I'll admit, I was a bit worried about what that might entail, but he has been a perfect gentleman.' She smirked briefly. 'Of course, that could be because he can't remember there's an alternative . . .'

'Does he still have our stone?' said Grace. 'The one you stole from us?'

Sally didn't look even a little bit embarrassed, because she doesn't do that.

'Honestly, darling, it wasn't like I had any choice. You've met psycho daughter and her wacked-out husband.' She glowered back the way we'd come. 'Are you sure Lex and his little dancing queen will be able to cope with them?'

'Polly is a werewolf, and Lex is the Damned,' I said. 'What about the stone?'

'It's here somewhere!' said Sally. 'I haven't seen it in ages, but I'm sure Leland will know where it is.'

'But if we're locked in . . .' said Grace.

'Please,' I said. 'Remember who you're talking to. I can handle locks.'

'And if you can't?' Grace said sweetly.

'Then you'll just have to charm them,' I said.

Sally snorted loudly. 'Best of luck with that. The door is on a time lock that can't be overridden because it's controlled by the computers. Psycho daughter really doesn't want her father running around loose.'

I looked at her. 'She's that scared of him?'

'I think more of what might happen when the song gets out of the stone,' said Sally. 'I know they definitely didn't want him to have it.'

Grace looked to me. 'What could be so dangerous about a song?'

'The sirens' song killed everyone who heard it, apart from Odysseus,' I said. 'Legend has it that the sirens were wiped out, just to make sure their song died with them. Leland and his computers could be bringing something unspeakably dangerous back into the world. A song that destroys the mind . . .'

Grace looked at him steadily. 'Do we really want this stone back?'

'We don't want Leland to have it,' I said. 'Besides, it's not like there's anything else here worth taking.'

'Then you'd better get a move on, darling,' said Sally. 'It can't be long now before the computers finish digging out the song.'

'Call to Leland,' I said. 'Let him know you're here.'

Sally shrugged and yelled his name, but there was no response. She scowled around her. 'Sometimes I think that man is deliberately hiding from me.'

'Really?' Grace said innocently. 'Why would he want to do that?'

'Tell me, Sally,' I said quickly, 'How were they able to grab you in Paris?'

'It wasn't my fault!' she said loudly. 'I was just lounging around, trying to find something worth watching on French television, when the door burst open and someone shot me with a tranquilizer dart. Next thing I know, I'm in another hotel room, not nearly as nice, and they've bolted this nasty collar around my throat.'

She pushed back the top of her blouse to reveal a thick steel band. I reached out to examine it, and Sally quickly backed away.

'Not a good idea, darling. There's a bomb attached. Set to explode if I try to remove the collar or make a run for it. You didn't think I stuck around here to be a good girl by choice, did you?'

'A remote-controlled bomb, to make you behave . . .' Grace smiled at me. 'Why did we never think of that?'

'Play nicely, children.' I leaned in close so that I could study Sally's collar without touching it. 'Can't you switch out the bomb for something else?'

'First thing I thought of, darling,' said Sally. 'But I can't seem to lock on to the explosive.'

'Hush!' said Grace. 'Someone's coming . . .'

A grey-haired old man in a grubby lab coat wandered out from behind a tall bank of equipment. Tall and thin, though bent over by the weight of his years, he had the look of a man who was always thinking of something else. He came to a halt, blinked at us a few times and then nodded easily, apparently not all that surprised or concerned to discover strangers in his studio.

'Ah, Sally, there you are. I was wondering where you'd got to. And you've brought friends to see me. How nice. My daughter doesn't normally allow me visitors; she doesn't want my work interrupted. Have you come to hear the sirens sing?'

'Hello, Leland,' I said politely. 'Actually, we're here to take Sally home.'

'Is it that time already?' said Leland. 'I do seem to lose track of things when I'm working.'

'Where is the stone, darling?' Sally said carefully. 'You know, the one with the song inside?'

'Hooked up to the computers,' said Leland. 'Took me ages to install it properly. Did you want to show it to your friends? I'm afraid they'll have to wait until the program has finished running. It shouldn't take long now.'

I nodded to Grace to move a little away, so we could talk privately.

'I don't think we're going to get the stone back,' I said quietly. 'Not unless we take this whole room apart with a crowbar.'

'Do we really want it?' said Grace. 'If Leland's computers remove the song, it's not going to be worth anything. You know . . . He seems harmless enough. Not at all what I was expecting.'

'Coldheart was just another of Murray's lies,' I said.

'There'll be no muttering in here, if you please!' Leland said loudly. 'Anything that can't be said in a clear and normal voice probably isn't worth listening to!'

Grace and I looked round. Leland was frowning at us severely. Sally made big placatory gestures behind his back, so I offered Leland my most polite smile.

'Sorry about that,' I said. 'We didn't want to disturb you. If Sally's ready, we'll be on our way.'

'Of course,' said Leland. He smiled cheerfully at Sally. 'Off you pop, dear. Don't let me keep you.'

'But first, we need you to tell the computers to open the studio door for us,' said Grace.

Leland shook his head. 'If the computers have locked the door, it's to make sure the song stays in here with me. They won't open the door again until it's finished. My daughter's idea. She doesn't want my great moment interrupted.'

'Can't you ask your daughter to open it?' I said.

'Oh, there's no communication with the outside,' Leland said cheerfully. 'It's all to do with security, you see.' He smiled at us, but his eyes were oddly distant. 'The song is all that matters.'

'Why?' said Grace.

'I'm fascinated by music,' said Leland. 'Down the years, I have heard it all, from songs to symphonies, ancient and modern. I only have one ambition left: to hear something no one else has heard for millennia. To know, at last, what song the sirens sang. Soon, my computers will play it for me.'

'How soon?' said Grace.

'Oh, any time now,' said Leland.

Grace and I looked at each other. Sally didn't like what she saw in our faces. She turned to Leland.

'Is there an off-switch, darling? Or a pause button?'

'Why would I want something like that?' said Leland. He was still smiling at us, but I couldn't see any humour in it. 'Did my precious daughter tell you I was senile and needed to be looked after? Nonsense. She insisted on the door because she's scared of the song.'

'She could have a point,' I said carefully. 'That song has killed most of the people who heard it.'

'I know!' said Leland. 'Exciting, isn't it? But I have to hear the song and understand the mystery of it at last. It's all I have left.'

'But . . . we're trapped in here with you!' said Sally. 'We could die!'

'Then you shouldn't have brought your friends in here to bother me, should you?' said Leland.

'How can you say that?' said Sally. 'After everything I've done for you!'

Leland's smile didn't waver. 'You don't matter. People don't matter. The song is everything.'

'Coldheart,' I said.

One of the machines made a loud chiming noise. Leland's smile widened.

'We're almost there . . .'

I followed his gaze to a computer screen, where a display was counting down from five minutes.

'Just enough time for me to find a comfortable chair,' said Leland, and he disappeared behind the wall of equipment again.

I turned quickly to Grace. 'Can you use your gift on the computers? Make them fall in love with you and stop the countdown?'

'I'm trying!' she said, glaring wildly around her. 'But they're not listening to me! Leland has all his computers working at full capacity. They can't accept any new input until they've played the song!'

'We have to get out of here!' said Sally.

She raced back to the studio door, with first me and then Grace practically treading on her heels. Sally beat on the solid steel with her fists and screamed at the top of her voice.

'*Let us out of here!*'

I took her by the shoulders and eased her firmly to one side. 'The door is soundproofed, remember?'

'But we can't stay here!' said Sally. 'I don't want to hear some song that will make my brains dribble out of my ears!'

'You're the one who understands locks, Gideon,' said Grace. 'Do something!'

I prised open some of the door's inner panels, so I could get a good look at the time-lock mechanism.

'Are you sure you know what you're doing?' said Grace.

'I'm a master thief, remember?'

'Only because you stole the title.'

'Doesn't that prove my point?'

'Concentrate, Gideon!'

I shook my head and stepped back from the door. 'This is a really sophisticated time lock, and I don't have the tools. Try your gift on it.'

'I can't! The lock takes its orders from the studio computers, and they're all busy concentrating on the song!'

I frowned, thinking hard. Grace and Sally kept their eyes fixed on me, trying to seem hopeful rather than desperate. I thought back on the long road this case had taken to get us here. And then I smiled.

'You've got a plan!' said Grace.

I took out my time pen. 'Remember how the pen's energies short-circuited the chain anchoring Tommy Two Way? Let's see what they can do to a time lock!'

I jammed the pen into the exposed mechanisms, and they sparked and sputtered as the energies in the pen overwhelmed them. The lock disengaged, and the door started to swing open. We forced our way past it, and the moment we were outside, all three of us put our shoulders to the door and used our combined weight to force it shut again. Just as the song began.

I only heard the first few notes before the soundproofed door cut them off, but I knew I would remember them for the rest of my life.

NINE
The Song Is Over

We left the warehouse and went back to the others. Fortunately, it seemed peace had broken out in our absence. Lex and Polly (still in her wolf form), Cleopatra and Mal were all chatting cheerfully together. They nodded easily as we came over to join them.

'We agreed on a truce,' said Lex. 'On the grounds that we didn't have anything worth fighting over.'

'And not at all because they were frightened of the Damned,' said Polly.

Sally threw herself into Lex's arms and hugged him fiercely. Lex patted her shoulder comfortingly and looked at me.

'Would I be right in assuming that things didn't go entirely as planned?'

'Coldheart's computers unlocked the sirens' song,' I said. 'They started to play it, but we got out just in time.' I gave Cleopatra a stern look. 'It would have been a lot easier if the studio door hadn't locked us in there.'

'Sorry about that,' said Cleopatra. 'I had Mal install the time lock in case it became necessary to seal my father in with the song.'

'He isn't senile, is he?' said Grace.

'No,' said Cleopatra. 'I just didn't want to admit that there is something wrong with my father.'

'There's a reason Murray gave him the name Coldheart,' I said.

'He's a heartless piece of shit,' said Mal.

'He's my father,' said Cleopatra.

'So you kept him locked up?' said Grace.

'It was either that or kill him,' said Mal.

Cleopatra nodded to Sally, who had finally let go of Lex and was taking an interest in the conversation again. 'Sorry we couldn't just let you go, but we needed someone for my father to talk to. It was one of the few things that kept him stable, and he'd stopped listening to me and Mal.'

'We hoped if we could keep him calm long enough, he might forget about the song and move on to something less life-threatening,' said Mal.

Sally glared at them and turned to Lex. 'I want them stamped on, hard! They strapped a bomb to my neck, to control me!'

'Really?' said Polly. 'What a marvellous idea . . .'

'One more word,' Sally said dangerously, 'and I will wait until you're asleep and shave rude words into your fur.'

'There isn't any bomb,' said Cleopatra. 'The collar's a fake. Always was.'

'We had to do something to make sure you wouldn't try to leave,' said Mal.

Sally gaped at them for a moment. 'That's why I couldn't switch out the explosive! Because it wasn't there! Do you have any idea what it was like, believing a bomb could blow my head off at any moment?'

'You're Switch It Sally,' said Cleopatra. 'You must have done something to deserve it.'

'Would you have stayed if we'd just asked you to?' said Mal.

'That's not the point!' Sally said loudly.

Lex carefully slipped his fingers inside the steel collar and tore it apart. He crumpled the metal pieces in his hands and threw them away. Sally glared triumphantly at Cleopatra and Mal. She never was a good winner.

Cleopatra kept her gaze fixed on me. 'I had Mal bring you the rock, in the hope it would disappear among all the other weird stuff in Old Harry's Place.'

'But why steal it back?' said Grace. 'After going to such trouble to leave it with us?'

'Murray must have been keeping an eye on what was happening,' said Mal. 'He told the old man where his precious stone was, and Leland insisted that we go and get it back.'

'And you went along with this?' said Grace. 'Even though you know how dangerous it was for him to have the rock?'

Cleopatra shrugged. 'He's my father.'

'If you've all quite finished messing about,' said a loud, familiar voice, 'perhaps we could get the hell out of here?'

We all looked round, to see a standing mirror wheeling itself towards us on squeaky castors.

'Sidney?' I said. 'Is that you?'

'Damn right it is. I am back! And it only goes to show just how much trouble you can get into when I'm not around to look after you.'

'How did Murray get rid of you?' I said.

'Wild goose chase,' the mirror said quietly. 'Don't want to talk about it.'

'What happened to Albert?' said Grace.

Sidney made a disgusted sound. 'The less said about him the better. There's always a black sheep in every family. Now, are you done here? Because I really would like to shake the dust of this place from my frame.'

'Just a little unfinished business first,' I said. I looked back at the warehouse. 'The song must be over by now.'

Cleopatra got out her phone. 'Let me check. I have an app that lets me know what's going on inside the studio. For when I couldn't be there with him.'

'Like a baby monitor?' said Grace.

'Sort of,' said Cleopatra. 'The computers have shut down . . . and I've just unlocked the studio door. We can go in now.'

For a long moment, nobody moved.

'You don't have to come with me,' I said.

'You heard the mirror,' said Lex. 'You need someone to look after you.'

'And if the Damned is going, I'm going,' said Polly. 'It's a family thing.'

'This is going to take some getting used to,' said Sally.

In the end, I made myself head back to the warehouse, and everyone else followed after me.

Apart from Sidney.

When we got to the studio door, it was standing wide open. I stopped a respectful distance away and listened carefully. I couldn't hear anything. I braced myself and led the way in. There wasn't a whisper of sound on the air, and the computers just blinked silently back at us. Mal moved over to the nearest keyboard and quickly started shutting everything down.

'I'm wiping all memory of the song the sirens sang,' he said. 'And when we're done here, I'll retrieve the rock, smash it into dust and scatter it to the four winds. Just in case. There's usually a good reason why things get forgotten.'

'There must be more rock from the island,' I said.

'What we had was a one-off,' said Cleopatra. 'Courtesy of Murray. I wouldn't even know where to look for more.'

'Just as well,' I said.

I went behind the wall of equipment where I'd seen Coldheart disappear and came back out pushing him on a swivel chair. He was sitting quietly, his gaze far away. Cleopatra said his name, but he didn't respond.

'He can't hear you,' I said. 'He can't hear anything but the sirens' song. I think he's going to be listening to that for the rest of his life.'

Grace looked at Cleopatra. 'Why didn't you just take the stone away from him?'

'He wanted to hear the song,' said Cleopatra. 'And it wasn't like he had anything else.'

'We had to go through the motions of stopping you,' said Malice, 'or he might have become suspicious and discovered the safety checks we'd put in place.'

'At least this way he'll die happy,' said Cleopatra.

'And you get to inherit all his treasures,' I said.

Cleopatra let out a bark of laughter. 'What treasures? He sold everything he had, to pay for all this nonsense.' She nodded to her husband. 'We can finally leave the undercity.'

'It's about time,' said Mal. 'Be nice to see a sky you can't bang your head on.'

Polly glared at me. 'I was promised as much treasure as I could carry away!'

I gestured around me. 'Feel free to take anything you want.'

Polly's fur bristled dangerously. 'So I walk away from this with nothing?'

'You have me,' said Lex.

'And me,' Sally said sweetly.

'This is going to take some getting used to,' said Polly.

Grace slipped her arm through mine. 'Can we go home now?'

'I don't see why not,' I said. 'You know the show's over when the bird women have finished singing.'